T5-ASB-112

The Library

of

Indiana Classics

The Ways of Furnessville. Gramp and Gram
as they appeared in their late-seventies.

DUNE BOY

The Early Years of a Naturalist

By

EDWIN WAY TEALE

Illustrated by

EDWARD SHENTON

Indiana University Press
Bloomington & Indianapolis

Published by arrangement with Dodd, Mead & Company, New York

Manufactured in the United States of America

Library of Congress Cataloging-in-Publication Data

Teale, Edwin Way, 1899-
  Dune boy.
  (The Library of Indiana classics)
  Reprint. Originally published: New York: Dodd, Mead, 1943.
  1. Teale, Edwin Way, 1899- . 2. Naturalists—
Indiana—Biography. I. Title. II. Series.
QH31.T4A3 1986 508.32'4 [B] 86-45957
ISBN 0-253-11860-3
ISBN 0-253-20421-6 (pbk.)

Dedicated To

My Grandparents

EDWIN AND JEMIMA WAY

With Gratitude

Which Has Grown With

The Years

CONTENTS

CONTENTS

LONE OAK—FORTY YEARS AFTER

DUNE BOY

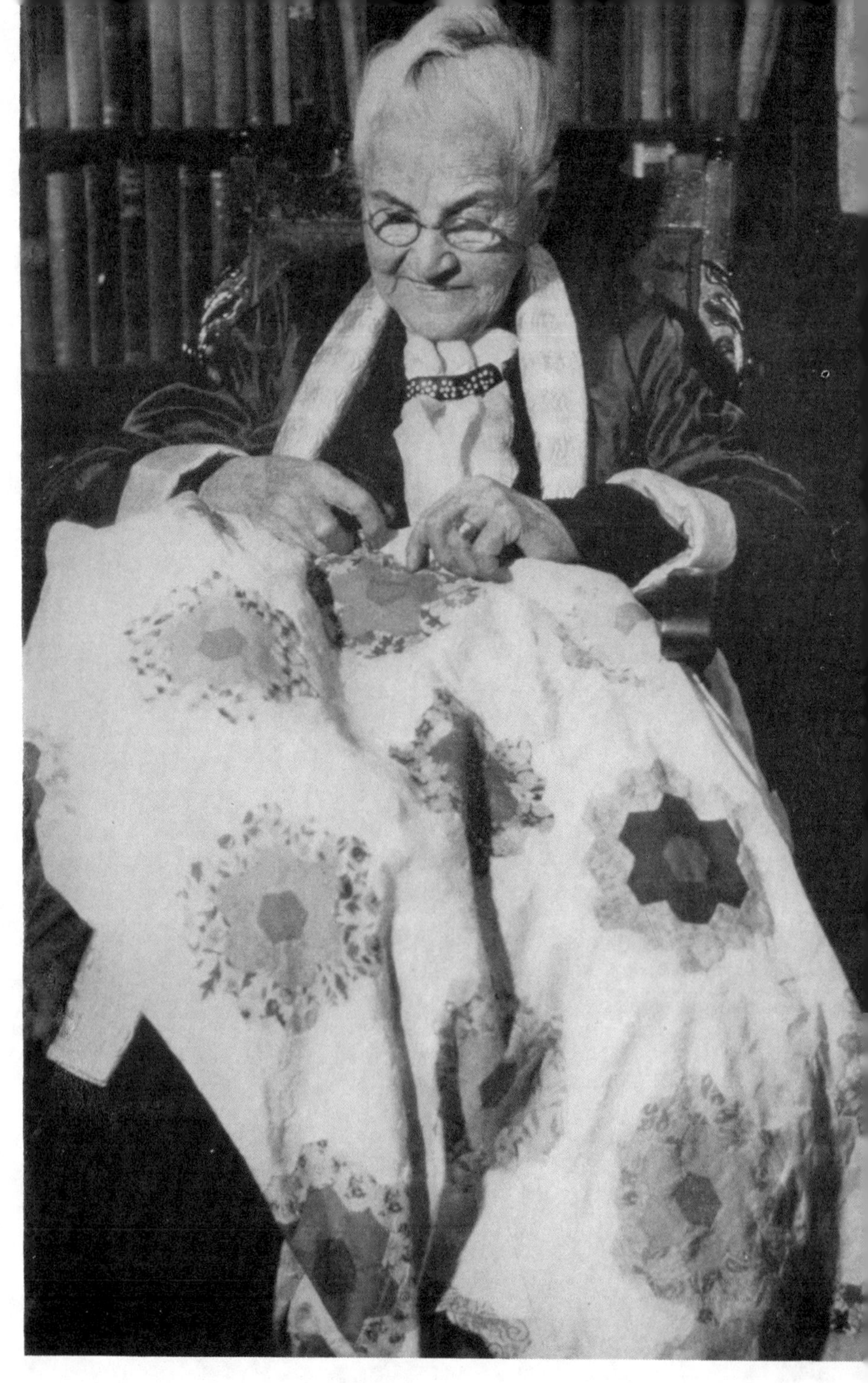

Jemima Way sewing on a quilt. At the time this photograph was made Gram was in her eighty-second year.

·1·

FAR DUNES

ACROSS the soot-stained and mossy roof of a low farmhouse, a narrow streak angled upward like the thin trail of a garden slug. It started at the lower edge of the kitchen roof, where a melon-crate leaned against the side of the house, and extended to the ridgepole of the dwelling. The trail was the product of innumerable scuffings and clingings. At its far upper end, a small boy, bareheaded and clad in blue overalls, hugged the peak of the farmhouse and gazed into the north.

The sun pressed its heat on his back; poured its heat on the ancient shingles around him. The smell of a pitchy tanarack tree was strong in the air. Mud-dauber wasps droned past on blurring wings, going and coming in their labors beneath the eaves. The countryside lay still in the heat of the midsummer morning.

A mile and a half away, across woods and swamps, the boy could see hills of gold shining in the sun. They were the crests of the great Indiana dunes which lifted their mountains of wind-blown sand above the level of the Lake Michigan shore. High above him, sliding along the blue of the sky, a bald eagle soared in their direction. The boy, squinting upward, followed its flight. Lower down, and passing directly over the white-and-green farmhouse, a gray sandhill crane flapped by, riding on six-foot wings and trailing its awkward legs, rudder-like, behind it.

The boy lay still in the sunshine. With his head on his hands, he watched the two great birds shrink in size. In his mind, he began to picture how the farm and the marsh and the distant dunes must appear to the eagle and the crane. His eyes again sought the far dunes. They rose like a shining, mysterious land of gold beyond the treetops. Hardly more than fifty miles from America's second-largest city, that stretch of lonely sandhills was a fragment of untamed wilderness. The boy had heard that wolves still howled among the snow-clad dunes on winter nights.

It was only in later years that he learned the history of this world beyond the treetops: how in a distant past bluffs had eroded into the waves on the western shore of Lake Michigan; how currents set up by the prevailing winds had carried the quartz grains to the southeastern tip of the lake where wind and wave and ice had forced them out onto the shore to create the almost fluid hills of the dune country. There, they formed a strange, tormented battleground where the wind and the root were ever at war—the wind striving to move the sand along, the vegetation seeking to anchor it down. Sometimes the wind won and, year after year, a sand-mountain moved ponderously forward, engulfing, like a glacier of quartz, the plants, the bushes, and even the trees which lay in the path of its advance. Again, this tug-o'-war ended in triumph for the root and a wandering dune became stationary, carpeted with green.

If the boy had viewed these sandhills from the altitude of the eagle, they would have had the appearance of a curving chain of green and golden beads. If he had seen them from the winding sand-road which skirted the bordering swamp, instead of from his more distant rooftop, the great hills would have resembled stooping giants, facing toward the east. Shaped by the prevailing wind from the northwest, their longer slopes were toward the west, their more abrupt descents toward the east. The dunes themselves, as well as the great blowouts and the small ribbed patterns on the beach sand, were autographs of the wind. But, to the boy, clinging to the rooftop in the hot sunshine, it was not the history of these sandhills which attracted him. It was the mystery of the far-away and the wildness of the dunes which stirred his imagination.

It was thus, as the boy in the blue overalls, that I spent many hours during the long summer days of my earliest boyhood.

Always, just west of my rooftop perch, I could see the bulk of an immense white oak. It towered a hundred feet into the air. Standing by itself, it gave my grandfather's farm its name: Lone Oak. I used to look up and up along the sheer rise of its great bole. The oak seemed propped against the sky. On days when the upper branches stood out against a background of drifting clouds, the old tree sometimes appeared to be moving, swinging in an arc toward me. I remember that once the impression became so overpowering that I scrambled away in a panic down the roof-slope.

The old farmhouse at Lone Oak stood at almost the exact physical center of the ninety-odd acres of marsh and woods and sandy soil which comprised my grandfather's farm. From my lookout I could see this farm spread out around me: the apple orchards; the rye fields; the asparagus patch; the red barn and the granary and the outbuildings; the straggling sand-road which appeared over a hill to the west, ran past the front gate of Lone Oak, and disappeared amid woods to the east; the swampy south pasture with its crisscrossing trails and its small elevated tract we called the Island; and, below the Island, the tracks of the Père Marquette Railroad, running east and west and forming the southern boundary of the farm. Beyond, away to the south—across a wide valley of low-lying farms and marshland—the blue hills of the Valparaiso moraine rose against the lighter blue of the summer sky.

Inch by inch, I knew our farm. I knew its chip-laden woodyard where I collected kindling and gathered stove-wood for the kitchen range. I knew its vast mow where I jumped from beams into the hay, sending up multitudes of glinting motes of dust. I knew its ditches, their sides filled with the massed green of juicy spearmint. I knew its spring where horses drank from a mossy trough formed of a hollowed-out poplar log. I knew its north woods, a mysterious realm of little trails and piles of yellow sand dug from burrows, and its even more mysterious marsh-lands, with their stagnant waters, their tangled vegetation, and their strange inhabitants.

Compared with the black loam of the riverbottom or the productive acres of the prairie, Lone Oak Farm probably was an unpromising tract. But to a boy, alive to the natural harvest of birds and animals and insects, it offered boundless returns.

Life, during these early years, was divided into a kind of mental Arctic night and day. During winter months, I lived in a city, went to school, moved in a crepuscular and foreign realm. Summers, and at Christmas, Thanksgiving and Easter vacations, I covered the seventy miles which separated Joliet, Illinois, from this dune-country farm of my grandparents.

That seventy miles seemed to carry me to the other side of the world.

At Lone Oak there was room to explore and time for

adventure. A new world opened up around me. During my formative years, from earliest childhood to the age of fifteen, I spent my most memorable months here, on the borderland of the dunes.

·2·

DUNE BOY

THE earliest Lone Oak visit that I can recall occurred at Christmastime when I was four years old. I have a vague remembrance of climbing down from the train at Furnessville; of the station lamps gleaming on the snow; of my grandfather, bundled in a fur coat until he resembled a great grizzly bear, holding high his lantern as he helped us into a low bob-sled while the horses stamped and jingled their sleigh-bells and sent out clouds of silver steam into the cold night air.

At the farmhouse, a Christmas tree, brought in from the woods, caught my eye. It was trimmed with polished apples, strings of popcorn, paper decorations and marshmallow fish. One of the latter, a four-inch pink fish dangling from one of the lower boughs, had a flavor which haunted me for years afterwards. To this day I have no idea what the flavor was.

As I grew older I developed into a gangling, rather long-nosed boy with gray-brown eyes, a vivid imagination, an extremely active but undisciplined mind, and a great love for the out-of-doors. My parents were sincere, hard-working, religious people. They tended to be conciliatory and gentle. The world, without doubt, would be a better place if all the people in it possessed their attributes. But, unfortunately, they do not. And the ones that do not invariably seem to prey upon the ones that do.

At home I was trained for Heaven rather than for the world as it is. My father worked in the Michigan Central roundhouse and we lived near the railroad tracks on Washington Street. My associates were boys given to fisticuffs. I was taught that it is wrong to fight. Being tall for my age and peaceably inclined, I was the target for most of the bullying of the neighborhood.

For years I worried a good deal over the fact that I didn't seem to have any temper. I could take a tremendous amount of punishment, refusing to give in. But rage and fury seemed to have been trained out of me. One day I overheard a neighbor woman discussing a boy with an ungovernable temper.

"When he's mad," she said, "he laughs instead of cries. And that is the sign of the most violent tempers of all!"

I thought the next time I was jumped on, I would let out a blood-curdling laugh and frighten my opponent out of his wits. I even practiced in secret before a mirror, screwing up my face into terrifying contortions and raising my laugh to a higher and higher pitch.

There was no long delay in finding an opportunity to try out the scheme. The very next time I was sent to the store my chief tormentor stepped out from an alley, brandishing his fists. I stood my ground and prepared to reveal my ungovernable temper by laughter. But, before I could open my mouth, I received a terrific wallop on the right eye and all thoughts of laughing deserted me.

Besides the handicap of feeling I was doing something wicked if I fought back, I had the additional obstacle of a sublime faith in the spoken word. When my father or mother told me anything, I could bank on it. They wouldn't say it unless it was true. Consequently, when some blustering boyhood opponent would assert that he would flatten my nose out on my face, I thought it was as good as flattened. My unrestrained imagination would present a clear picture of my face without a nose. It was only in the course of time that I learned the ways of the world and practical modes of procedure.

In those harried days of early grade-school I got along as best I could. I retired within myself and much of the time lived in a dream-world of my own making. In fifth grade a temporary attack of deafness added to my difficulties for more than half a year. Thus it was that the freedom of Lone Oak made the place a sort of Never-Never-

Land come true. I used to cross off the days on the calendar and count the number remaining before the next vacation when I would return again to the green pastures of that Indiana farm.

Even as I lived them I had a feeling of the infinite preciousness of those early days, a feeling of trying to hold back the clock and enjoy to the full each passing second. In later years I could always beguile tedious hours by reliving moments selected at random from this period of the past. Many times in distress or pain or discouragement, in dentist's chairs and operating rooms, I have diverted my mind with thoughts of Lone Oak. How profound must have been the impressions of those sunrise days to have left a mark so lasting!

My grandparents gave me all the freedom I needed. There was health for the mind as well as for the body at Lone Oak. I was, during that period, inclined to fits of sullenness. I was never permitted to talk back at home; to say "I won't" was unthinkable. My only outlet for willfullness was sulking. At Lone Oak the moodiness and sullenness, which might have become ingrained, were dissipated by the healthful outdoor activity and the freedom from restraint.

I had the feeling then, as each generation of boys undoubtedly has and will have, that the generation before had seen all the great sights and that only minor occurrences were left for me to witness. On summer evenings, beside a smudge fire which kept the mosquitoes at bay, my grandfather would tell me tales of the early days, the Indians, the wolves, the deer, the struggles of the pioneers. Immense stretches of land now devoted to corn and oats, melons and potatoes, had been covered with forest when he came west. The stories I heard from his lips on those summer evenings or when we rested in the shade from hoeing or as we jolted along the sand-roads on our way to town were like windows looking back into a glorious and adventurous past.

But there was, in the dune country of my day, much to see and much to enjoy. I was out-of-doors from morning until night, running barefoot and in overalls, a straw-hat protecting me from the midday sun. Capable of tremendous enthusiasms, I was like a dog that has lost the scent—darting first this way, then that. One day I would be head over heels in one activity, the next day just as excited about another. Undoubtedly I led my grandparents a merry chase. They rarely knew what was coming next. One time they would discover me making a harness out of binding-twine for a baby calf; another time I would have plans all worked out for devoting the whole farm to cabbage and shipping trainloads to Chicago. I remember how vividly I could see, in my mind's eye, a puffing locomotive and a long line of freight cars stretching away to the horizon and a banner on each carrying the sign: "Lone Oak Cabbages."

In William Butler Yeats' poetic play, *The Land of Heart's Desire,* one of the characters observes:

> "For life moves out of a red flare of dreams
> Into a common light of common hours
> Until old age brings the red flare again."

Thus it was that my grandparents seemed to understand, best of all, the world of dreams, of fantastic plans, of make-believe in which I spent so many hours.

When we are young we know least of all how different we are, or how different from the norm are those around us. It takes perspective to see ourselves in relation to the world at large. It was only after many years had passed that I understood how strange a boy I must have been or how unusual were the two who were my closest summer companions. As remarkable as the dune country itself, as remarkable as the varied fields of the farm from which they had so long wrung a living were these two old people—my grandparents, the Ways.

·3·

THE WAYS

WHEN memory began for me my grandfather was well past sixty—a great, bearded man, six feet one inch tall, raw-boned and gnarled. His unruly thatch of hair, which remained with him until the time of his death at the age of eighty-five, was streaked with its earliest gray. He had black eyes and a straight nose which ended in a slightly flattened tip. Once he explained gravely to me that he got that flattened tip as a small child when he fell down and stepped on his nose.

The laughing wrinkles which puckered the outer corners of his deep-set eyes were not accidental. They were the product of a kindly and humorous nature. The ax and the hoe and the pitchfork, the years of toil which had bowed his shoulders and enlarged the knuckles of his hands, had never dulled his sense of humor nor his love of a joke.

"Edwin," he used to say, "run up t' th' house an' git me a drink o' water an' I'll give y' th' first silver dollar I find rollin' uphill!"

As a teller of tales, stories of the frontier days and of his adventures in the Civil War, he was superlative. He had a gift for the colorful phrase, the humorous twist, the original observation. His voice was soft and of a remarkable timbre. Many of his stories centered in the doings of a mythical "Mr. Bump." His most preposterous tales always ended in the same manner:

"That's th' way 't happened, so help me Thirty-Six!"

Who, or what, Thirty-Six was nobody knew.

Wherever he went "Gramp"—as I always called him—made friends without apparent effort. He had a genius for getting himself invited to dinner. Once, in the early days of hard sledding at Lone Oak, he was called to serve on the jury at Valparaiso. The best trousers he owned were worn out at the knees and Gram had to patch them with material of a different kind. In spite of the social handicap of patched trousers, Gramp—on the day that the trial was over—was invited to dine at the home of the judge.

I have before me a letter written home during the Civil War by one of his brothers. It says in part: "Ed's getting along fine. He goes out in the country and makes friends with the first citizen he comes to and stays to dinner." At the end of half an hour you felt you had known Gramp all your life. When my mother was a very small girl she once asked him:

"How long were you and I here before Mother came?"

That feeling that Gramp had been a friend from the beginning is one that can be best understood only by those who knew him.

I early learned at Lone Oak that he had an aversion to giving orders. He hated to be bossed or bullied and he respected a similar sentiment in others. He tempered his orders so they sounded like suggestions. But the meaning was the same.

One July morning, as he was leaving to cultivate the south cornfield, he said:

"Edwin, y' kin pick up th' 'tatoes in th' west patch t'day ef you've a mind t'."

Then he clucked to his horses and drove out of the barnyard. The day wore on and I didn't have a mind to pick up potatoes. Evening came and the tubers were still in the field. Gramp, dusty and tired, unhitched the team and led them down to the watering trough. I trailed behind to watch the frogs in the mossy depths of the well.

"How many bushels o' 'tatoes was they?" Gramp inquired.

"I don't know."

"Well, how many did y' pick up?"

"I didn't pick up any."

"Not any! Why in blazes not?"

"Well, you said to pick them up if I had a mind to. You didn't say I had to."

In the next few minutes I learned once and for all that when Gramp said I could if I had a mind to, it also meant that I had better have a mind to.

Born in 1842 on a farm in Chemung County, in upstate New York, Gramp had been christened Edwin Franklin Way. His mother died when he was twelve years old and the family, consisting of his father, his two sisters, and two brothers, migrated west to Indiana. They settled in the dune country in 1854, the year that the Michigan Central Railroad reached Chicago.

Until he was a soldier in the Civil War, Gramp never wrote a letter in his life. Then he had a comrade help him with the spelling. Even after one of his daughters was the wife of a college president, he still blithely ignored the dictates of Webster and the grammarians. So far as I know, he never knew how to make a capital I. He always referred to himself in the lower case. He never read a book until after he was married. Yet, although his formal education in frontier country schools ended almost before it began, he was a living refutation of that specious fallacy of the literate—the belief that illiteracy and ignorance are synonymous.

Gramp was one of those unschooled men whose minds are not molded to a conventional pattern. He was always himself, never anyone else. His ideas had matured gradually, unhurriedly. They had not been forced in a hothouse of learning. They were sun-ripened. His casual remarks were often fresh, humorous and flavorsome. They smacked of his own personality.

"Those pants," he said one day when my trousers had shrunk in the wash, "look like they'd been picked too soon!"

When Gram remarked that a neighbor girl was sweet, Gramp declared: "I don't know whether she's sweet er not. I never tasted her."

"When y' git older," he observed on another occasion, "th' years keep goin' faster an' faster. Seems t' be Fourth o' July all th' year 'round."

Seen in retrospect, Gramp was probably not a very efficient farmer. Although it was he who introduced the growing of muskmelons into the dune country and although one farmer traveled more than fifty miles to get instructions from him, he often planted his crops without much of an eye to proper soils or rotation. He was a pioneer and set routine galled his spirit. He didn't like "fuss and feathers." He desired existence plain and simple. He wanted to "camp out" at home. At the table he was like Henry Thoreau: The dish he preferred was "the nearest."

A good joke was worth more than a dollar to Gramp. Not infrequently people took advantage of his good nature; imposed upon him by appealing to his sense of humor.

I remember one blistering July day when there was a knock at the front door just as we were sitting down to the noon meal. On the other side of the screen stood a disreputable-looking tramp.

"Might I have a bite to eat?" he asked. "I am willing to work at my trade to earn a meal."

"What is your trade?" Gramp inquired.

"I am," said the tramp with meekly downcast eyes, "an ice-cutter."

Gramp roared with laughter and heaping up a plate carried it out under a tree for the tramp to eat.

A joke on himself was as good as a joke on anybody else. For years he used to tell about the night he chased the cows through the corn.

Two young practical jokers of the neighborhood had waited until about midnight before appearing at Lone Oak with cowbells in their hands. Ringing the bells near Gramp's bedroom window, they worked gradually toward a near-by cornfield. Half asleep, Gramp pulled on his clothes and stumbled out into the night. The cows seemed to be at the far end of the field. He rushed in that direction. The bells rang tantalizingly a hundred yards away. He raced toward the sound. The cows weren't there. The sound of the bells came from a new direction. For half an hour he stumbled about in the darkness in pursuit of the phantom cattle. Finally he gave up. His shouting stopped. With a: "Blast ye! Go ahead an' founder yerselves!" he returned to the house.

The next morning the cows were peacefully munching their cuds in the barnyard. While he was scratching his head over this, a neighbor, going to town, reined up his horses.

"Ed," he called, "I hear y' had cows in yer corn las' night."

Then he drove on, chuckling to himself. Later in the morning, a second neighbor pulled up and inquired:

"Cows outa yer corn yit, Ed?"

As soon as he had disappeared around a bend in the road, Gramp made for the cornfield. Between the rows of standing corn there were no cow-tracks. But there were the footprints of running human feet. And most of the tracks had been made by other shoes than his own.

"What a big stand-up-and-fall-down!" he exclaimed. Then he returned laughing to the barnyard.

Under Gramp's good nature, however, there was no lack of spirit or courage. If anybody willfully or intentionally wronged him, he would "get up on his hind legs like a man" as he was wont to express it. In the days when a new ax took money that couldn't well be spared he once set a tramp to chopping up some kindling in payment for a meal. As soon as he wasn't watched, the come-along shouldered the ax and set off at a trot down the road. When Gramp discovered the tramp had stolen his ax, he started in hot pursuit.

Gram, seeing he was unarmed and thinking the tramp might attack him with the ax, ran after him, shouting for him to stop. Around the bend they came. The tramp looked back and saw Gramp, hatless and with his beard flying in the wind, bearing down on him with Gram, her sunbonnet clutched in her hand, a hundred yards behind.

"Drop that ax, y' scalawag!" Gramp bellowed.

The tramp obeyed. He sprinted wildly for the woods.

"But he might have killed you!" Gram remonstrated as they regained their breath and walked back to the farm.

"What d' y' think I'd a bin doin' about thet time?" Gramp wanted to know.

In her way, Gram was as remarkable as Gramp. She was only sixteen when she had come as his bride to Lone Oak Farm. They had arrived in a wagon drawn by Duke and Dime, Gramp's two pure-white oxen. The oxen were the only draft animals he possessed. In later years Gram used to tell how patient and beautiful and strong they were. Gramp remembered how confounded slow they were.

At the time of their marriage Gram, with her regular features, her masses of shining brown hair and the clear red of health in her cheeks, must have possessed singular beauty. All her life she washed her face only in water; she never used soap. And even when she was well past fifty, her skin retained its rose-petal softness. Five feet, five inches in height, she hardly came to Gramp's shoulder.

She had been born in Ogdensburg, N.Y., and had spent her early years near the banks of the St. Lawrence. Her maiden name was Jemima George. Her father, Henry George, was a prosperous masonry contractor, engaged in building large churches in the region. In her sixteenth year, while she was attending a select seminary for young ladies in Ogdensburg, her father lost both health and money in a sudden series of reverses. The family moved west to a farm a few miles from Lone Oak and there Henry George died two years later.

For the young girl, this swift change from the classics of the Ogdensburg schoolroom to the rough frontier society of the dune country in 1867 was like a plunge from daylight into darkness. On her first week in her new home she was invited to go to a prayer meeting at the Furnessville church. There she heard one of the women arise to announce:

"Brothering and sistering, I want t' testify an' thank th' Lord. I ain't seen th' man I'm a-feerd of yit!"

Bewildered and uncertain, shy and misunderstood, Gram had floundered about for several months. Then she met Gramp. At the time, he possessed nine white shirts —probably more than he owned at any one time in his whole later life—and was still arrayed for state occasions in the blue army overcoat he had brought home from the war. In the fall of 1867, when Gramp was twenty-five and Gram sixteen, they were married.

Those early days at Lone Oak were never easy. Malaria became so bad at times that a little dish of quinine was placed on the table and every member of the family had to dip out a quantity and swallow it at breakfast-time. Bending over her scrub-board or laboring at the churn, Gram would be wracked by chills and fever. When help was scarce she hoed under the blistering sun. She reared four children—a son, Allan, who died in early manhood; Clara, my mother; Winnifred, and Elizabeth. High-strung, sensitive, and comparatively frail, she was ill-fitted for the frontier life she led.

This hard labor which was her lot never broke her spirit. She had flint in her makeup. Sometimes the flint struck sparks. There were days when she was over-tired and irritable. Fatigue is Life's great poison. When we are thoroughly rested, how reasonable and agreeable we are! Angels may be angels because they can rest eternally. On days when Gram was over-worked and tart-tongued, Gramp would take me aside and say:

"Mother's got alum on 'er tongue this mornin'. Better steer clear o' th' kitchen."

At the time when her children were young and the drain on her strength was greatest, an event of lasting importance occurred in the community. The Township trustees purchased a set of 140 of the world's classic books of history and literature. They were bound in leather and housed in a special bookcase. Members of the community could take out books as from a public library. For many years these books remained at Lone Oak and Gram was their custodian.

She read aloud every one of the millions of words they contained. The books provided higher education at Lone Oak. She and Gramp knew all the great battles of history; they were familiar with the plays of Shakespeare and the poems of Milton and the novels of George Eliot. Biography interested them most of all. Gramp knew the life of Napoleon forward and backward.

For more than forty years Gram read aloud almost every evening and it was one of the big events of the day. Sometimes, in earlier years, neighbors or hired men from near-by farms used to stroll over after the chores were done to listen in on the reading. In summer they would stretch out on the front porch, puffing silently at their pipes and slapping now and then at a pestiferous mosquito. Beside a kerosene lamp, inside the screen door, Gram would read on and on, her expressive voice rising with the exciting passages.

Oftentimes Gram was emotional and impulsive. Once she threw the mop at a cat making tracks across her clean kitchen floor and then cried for half an hour because she hit it. Idealistically, she usually was right. She never compromised with the wickedness of the world. A wrong was a wrong to her no matter how gilded or sugar-coated. "It is wonderful," says Charles Dickens in his preface to *Oliver Twist*, "how Virtue turns from dirty stockings; and how Vice, married to ribbons and a little gay attire, changes her name, as wedded ladies do, and becomes Romance." But not for Gram. She saw through guile as through a window-pane. And she walked alone, if necessary.

"Part of our responsibility," she used to say, "is to keep evil-doers from doing evil. It isn't enough just to forgive them the evil they do!"

Another time she observed: "Most old ladies look to me like they had their mouths clamped shut to keep from saying what they really thought."

Neither moths nor old age corrupted the violence of her indignation against tyranny and oppression. The injustices of history, even those of a thousand years before, touched off her scorn and contempt just as much as did the injustices of her own day and community. The viewpoint of not caring what happened, so long as it didn't happen to her, was incomprehensible to Gram. She was an Isaiah in a sunbonnet. Single-handed, she was a society for the prevention of cruelty to animals and men. Wherever wrong and injustice reared their heads she was there in valiant spirit. You had the feeling that if the whole world crashed around her, she would fight on, solitary and alone.

Alongside her spirit of resolution for fair-dealing, Gram had a deep love of beauty. When she was nearing seventy-five, and had gone to live with one of her daughters, she spent a whole delightful morning washing chinaware after a social function simply because, as she said, the beautiful patterns on the dishes gave her pleasure. The birds, the flowers, the clouds—all that was beautiful around her—attracted her deeply. She was like the father of the French painter, Millet, of whom it is related that he used to pluck handfuls of grass and show them to his son, saying: "See how beautiful this is!"

The yard at Lone Oak was no ordinary place; it was no stretch of bare ground and straggling weeds. A terraced lawn ran from the front porch to the road. Flowers bordered the walk and roses were everywhere. There were lilacs, half a century old; flowering almonds; double hollyhocks; climbing nasturiums; peonies, and diamond-shaped beds of dahlias. I recall one of the first automobiles to churn through the sand of the road which passed the house. The driver halted in amazement and the people in the strange machine sat for a long time looking at the oasis of Gram's front yard. Finally the driver got out and offered me twenty-five cents—a great sum—for a bouquet of the flowers.

Gram cared for the yard in spare moments and in the cool of the evening after the day's work was over. Raising flowers provided an outlet for her nervous tension and for her intense love of the beautiful.

In a pioneer society it is the harder qualities of mind and character that are at a premium. The softer virtues are looked upon as luxuries. Men and women, struggling desperately to make ends meet, are like tightrope-walkers who cannot forget for a moment the business of preserving their lives. A sensitiveness to the color and poetry of Nature is unessential, excess baggage. Such people have an instinctive dread of luxuries. Their lives, of necessity, are spent stifling the desire for luxury. It is only the rare and superlative character who is able to retain the softer qualities, beneath his armor, in a world of constant struggle. This Gram did and she stands out in my mind as one of the indomitable, great women of my meeting.

She had her own fund of stories, many of them the product of her imagination. There was one summer, when I was very small, that she put me to sleep each night with a new installment of a continued story about the River Pixies. After the dishes were washed and while the chorus of the katydids and crickets was swelling outside the bedroom window, she would come and sit beside me and make up adventure after adventure while I listened entranced. Faint, long-ago images of little people, with peaked caps, running about the banks of a dark stream, remain with me still.

These, then, were the two people about whose lives I —their only grandson—whirled like a satellite from June to September in the golden days of summer and youth. My parents appeared from time to time at Lone Oak Farm. The daughters of the family came home often for part of the summer. But there were long stretches when we were alone, the three of us—two old and one young. The debt I owe my grandparents most of all is the freedom they gave me, freedom to roam the acres of corn and wheat and potatoes, the woods and swamps, and to make this world my own.

·4·

INDIAN DAYS

THE only shadow that saddened these early days was the fact that I had not been born an Indian.

As a boy, I used to think a great deal about it—contrasting my lot with the happy, carefree existence which would have been mine if I had been born in some Chippewa's wigwam. Then I would have lived a life remote from schoolbooks and dull routine; then my grown-up future would have been a long succession of sunlit years spent under the open sky. When I broached my dissatisfaction to Gramp, he said:

"Well, y' might ez well make up y'ur mind t' bein' a

paleface, Edwin, cuz it's too late t' do anythin' about it now."

Somehow I felt my father and mother were to blame for not being redskins. In various ways I sought to make up for the deficiency of being born with a white skin. I cultivated a dusky hue by washing as infrequently as the law, and Gram, would allow. I walked along a line with my toes pointing straight ahead in careful Indian-fashion. On one occasion I tried to live on acorns for a whole day. I patched together bits of leather and calico and rabbit fur into an amazing, multi-hued Indian jacket which alarmed even the cows and chickens.

One night I slept on the hard floor of the bedroom to toughen my body, and another day I walked around out of sight of the farmhouse for half an hour with a block of wood perched on my head in an effort to develop the straight-as-an-arrow posture of the noble red man. Then there was the August afternoon when I gave Gram a fright by appearing at the kitchen door with my face darkened with blackberry juice.

About this time I first heard someone discussing the idea of reincarnation. I became an immediate convert and was greatly cheered by the thought that I might have been an Indian, even a chief, during some previous existence. The summer that Ernest Thompson Seton's *Two Little Savages* fell into my hands I went rapidly from bad to worse. Chicken-feather head-dresses trailed down my back and flapped in the breeze and I rarely moved without being accompanied by my bow and quiver of arrows. Gramp had shaped the bow with a drawknife from a length of seasoned ash. But it was the arrows which were my special pride and joy. Their shafts were of oak and carefully polished and they were tipped with real Indian arrowheads, fashioned from flint.

At that time spearheads and tomahawk-heads and arrowheads were plowed up frequently from the sandy soil of the Lone Oak fields. Indians of various tribes had successively occupied the dune country. Mighty but forgotten battles had been fought over the very land where I now roamed.

Within a few minutes' walk of the farmhouse there lay a number of sites closely associated with earlier, more primitive days. These spots attracted me time after time. I used to make expeditions, for example, to a small patch of tangled woodland, clinging to the side of a sandhill. Here, Gramp had told me, the last Canadian lynx in the region had been killed the year that I was born. Another pilgrimage, as to some Mecca, carried me to the top of a rise which overlooked our lower meadow. In that field, one misty autumn morning long ago, Gramp had seen more than twenty deer feeding among his cattle. But the spot which most often drew me was the marshland "island" where Gramp's cows stood in the shade and flicked away flies with their tails during the hottest hours of the August noontide.

According to legend, this "island" had been a battlefield of the Indians. At any event, the sand which lay beneath the sparse grass was a storehouse, a museum, of

Indian implements. It was here that I obtained the flint tips for my arrows.

At one time I had more than 100 arrowheads, spear-heads and tomahawk-heads which I had picked up in this relatively small area. Whenever the Gunders plowed the field which bordered the "island" on the west, the plowshare brought to light an amazing number of flint arrowheads. As I hunted these reminders of unwritten history, I used to imagine myself in the thick of ancient battles. I used to wonder what the country looked like in those days, what game lived in herds and coveys among the hills and swamps of the dune country, what life-and-death struggles had taken place at the very spot where I was standing.

The most memorable moment in connection with these years of wishing I were an Indian came as the result of a stray bit of redskin lore which I encountered in a magazine article. It stated that young warriors showed their mettle by placing live coals on their wrists and letting them burn to ashes without flinching.

I determined to prove my courage with coals of fire.

That afternoon, when I was alone in the kitchen, I gingerly opened the hot door of the range and peered in. Tongues of red flames flicked and darted above a mass of glowing coals. The torrid breath of the fire struck me in the face. I hastily closed the door. The bottom had dropped out of my resolution.

It took five minutes of earnest and silent dialogue to bring my determination back to the sticking point and my paleface body back within reach of the stove. Poker in hand, I fished out a spitting coal of glowing red. It was fully as large as a quarter.

In the breeze of my excited breathing it dilated like a baleful red eye. It seemed to grow in size. I could see it in my imagination, searing the flesh with strong-smelling smoke curling up just as it did when the blacksmith clamped a red-hot shoe on Dolly's hoof. After consideration, I recalled that the item I had read had said nothing about the *size* of the coal. I decided to try a smaller one.

After considerable maneuvering, I succeeded in extracting a second coal. This one was about the size of a nickel. It still looked huge and hot—far too hot and far too huge. I pushed it back hastily and closed the door of the stove to rest my eyes and rally my moral forces. Next time the coal was hardly as large as a dime. To my great relief, it burned itself out and became merely a grayish lump, which rapidly lost its heat, before I was ready to transfer it to the bare skin of my wrist.

A final try—and this time courage triumphed.

I placed the live coal—which by the progression of events had become no larger than a soot flake—on my wrist. It glowed briefly and then expired like a falling star. When I examined the skin of my wrist, under the harsh sunshine outdoors, I detected a minute spot of red. The burn was of pinhead proportions. But it was, nevertheless, a self-inflicted burn, a badge of fortitude. I felt assured that, in spite of my paleface skin, I had the mettle of an Indian brave.

The next best thing to being an Indian, in my early dreams, was roving the northern woods as a Hudson Bay trapper. This ambition was kept alive by the successive arrivals of a bulky volume which held an honored place in dune-country homes. This was the Sears, Roebuck catalogue. It was no mere exhibit of wares for sale. It was infinitely more. It was a fabulous, farm-boy's book of dreams, a doorway into magical realms.

The section which held me entranced longest of all was devoted to sporting goods. Here I found tents and guns and canoes, cowboy hats and blacksnake whips, traps and lumberman's shirts and hunting boots. I read the all-too-short descriptions again and again. Like many children of that day, I learned to read largely by the Sears, Roebuck method—by trying to find all about the things I wanted most to own.

On winter evenings and during the heat of midsummer days, I used to beguile the time with imaginary journeys into the wilderness. On maps in an old *Montieth's Geography* I laid out courses and calculated mileages along the great rivers of the Northland—the Saskatchewan, the Athabaska, the Mackenzie.

Then would follow delightful hours with the Sears, Roebuck catalogue once more—leafing back and forth from the grocery section to the sporting goods section to the clothing section—listing all the staples required for the journey. Some of these old listings, made in those days, are still in existence. One includes, among other things, the following items, with the order numbers attached: 6K4053, Wolf Trap; 6K4089, Trap Setter; 6K4114, Tree Trap; 6K4230, Skin Tanner. When the lists were completed there would come the big moment when I would add up the figures and arrive at the grand total—the amount for which the imaginary trip actually could be made.

None of these trips up the rivers of the northern map ever materialized. Trapping among the white fastnesses of the Canadian wilderness remained a dream. But, for one brief period at Lone Oak, I did become a professional trapper. The record of that adventure, how it began and what its conclusion was, is the story of the succeeding pages.

·5·

MOUSE PELTS

THE granary at Lone Oak lifted its gray bulk above a small cluster of outbuildings. Set in an open space, this group of close-packed structures resembled an island of trees on the prairie. Just as such a grove often is dominated by its tallest tree, so the cluster was dominated by the towering form of the granary. It was second in size only to the barn itself.

Years of weathering had worn away the outer surface of its unpainted boards. Below every ancient nailhead a tiny rust-stalactite lay embedded in the wood. But the rough-hewn beams of the building's skeleton were as sturdy as ever. Within their framework, the interior was broken up into a central open space near the door and three roomlike bins—one for oats, one for wheat, one for rye. Overhead, among the rafters, a vast, dim storage space was haunted by mud-daubers and mice. Circling the walls of the open space, on a level with my head, a narrow shelf supported a regiment of small tobacco boxes, cigar boxes, and cheese boxes. They were filled to overflowing with nails and screws, wire and bolts, washers, bits of chain, and crumbs of tobacco—with the oddments of long accumulation.

This structure was far more than a storage place for rye and wheat and hardware. The granary was also a Rainy Day Club where Gramp and I foregathered and where he smoked his pipe and mended bits of harness and told me enthralling stories of his own boyhood.

At such times the air would be filled with a delicious variety of odors. The smell of the fresh rain pelting into the hot, dry dust outside the doorway would be mingled with the aroma of Gramp's corncob pipe, with the odor of paint and tar and axle-grease. Innumerable other olfactory ingredients contributed anonymously to the whole. But one predominant ingredient was far from anonymous. This was the all-pervading mousy smell which filled the interior of the old building.

For Gramp's granary was a kind of mouse sanctuary. Successive generations of squeaking rodents grew sleek and fat on the abundance which overflowed its bins. Their small black droppings, which Gramp referred to as "mouse seeds," were much in evidence. If we sat silent for a moment we could hear the scurrying of little feet below the floorboards or among the rubbish overhead. Sometimes the little animals would peer out from holes gnawed through the bottom-boards of the bins at the floor-line. Only their pointed noses, their quivering whiskers, their bead-black little eyes would be visible. Then, if we continued to remain unmoving, they would dart out across the floor with high-pitched squeaks to whisk out of sight again in other holes.

The way this mouse population took possession of his granary stirred Gramp, from time to time, to rare outbursts of wrath. One August day, when the bins were full and the harvest was over and word seemed to have been passed around so that mice from the fields were moving into the Promised Land, Gramp took action.

"Edwin," he said, "y' want to be trapper, don't y'?"

"I sure do!"

"Then why don't y' trap these pesky mice?"

"I haven't any traps."

"Well, next time we go t' town, I'll buy y' a bunch. Y' catch these mice and I'll give y' a nickel a dozen fer their tails."

The fact that that seemed a magnificent price offers eloquent testimony as to the mouse population of the granary. In fact, as I listened to the scurry and the squeaking of the various families encamped within the walls of the building—and emboldened by plenty and easy security—I concluded that here lay a smooth, broad highway to riches.

The next time we drove to Michigan City, Gramp was as good as his word. He bought two dozen spring mouse-traps at Staiger's Hardware and handed me the package as we left the store.

"Now yer in the trappin' business," he told me as we unhitched the horses and climbed into the cracker-wagon.

Hardly had the wheels stopped rolling in the Lone Oak barnyard before I was out establishing my trap-line. With fragments of cheese for bait, I distributed the spring-traps along the shelves and beams and near the black, gaping holes gnawed in the flooring. Before darkness came I already had a dozen slender little tails which I delivered to Gramp in triumph. With five pennies in "bounty money" jingling in my pocket, I reset the traps and prepared for bed. Unaware of any law of diminishing returns, I dreamed that night of an unending harvest of mouse-tails which would save Gramp's grain and fill my pockets with copper coins.

These rosy expectations seemed justified at dawn next morning. There was a mouse in every trap. As I ate a hearty breakfast of fried eggs and bacon, washed down with milk five minutes from its source, I counted up the days until I had to return to school and multiplied by ten to get the total of my revenue.

That day a new idea occurred to me. I would skin the mice and make little pelts of their soft fur. This work proved more delicate than I had anticipated but, after many whettings of my jackknife, I mastered the art of mouse-skinning and by evening had five little pelts drying on a board in the woodshed. Held in place with pins, each was well rubbed with salt and alum. Gramp and Gram came out to look at them after supper and Gram wondered "what I'd think of next."

It wasn't mouse-tails that I dreamed of that night. It was tiny pelts softer than velvet. In my imagination I had leaped ahead to a position as the John Jacob Astor of the Mouse Pelts. I could foresee a whole industry founded on mouse-skins. With no effort at all I could close my eyes and see bales and bales of tiny skins tied up, awaiting shipment in carload lots.

However, with the passing of a week, the daily catch began to taper off. In spite of their seemingly inexhaustible numbers, the granary mice were giving out. I tried bigger pieces of cheese, then other baits, then clusters of unbaited traps placed around every hole. I washed the traps and smoked them in approved trapper-fashion to remove human smell. In spite of everything, the take diminished day by day. I was discouraged. But Gramp was delighted.

"Y've jest about cleaned th' little varmints out!" he exulted.

"But I thought there were millions of mice!"

"They sounded like a million, all right," he agreed. "But y' can't always tell by sound. I rec'llect about Mr. Bump an' th' frogs. One summer th' frogs in a little pond near Mr. Bump's house croaked so much he couldn't sleep nights. He contracted with a hotel in th' city t' supply 10,000 pair o' frog-legs. When he tried t' deliver th' legs he couldn't find only eight frogs in th' whole pond. But they had sounded like 10,000 to him!"

I turned to other pelts, to gophers and moles and a red squirrel or two. Once, as we were returning home from Michigan City, I spied a dead rabbit along the road and, in spite of Gramp's remonstrances, brought it home to skin. Another time I raced across a field to the eastern orchard where Gram was picking up early harvest apples, with an SOS for alum. I had discovered a large discarded bacon rind and had it nailed up on the granary door ready for tanning. But my greatest source of oddity pelts was Rose-of-the-Army.

Rose-of-the-Army was our black and white mother cat. She was one of the greatest hunters I have ever met and, as her latest litter of kittens then was growing up, she appeared at frequent intervals with fresh quarry from the fields. Her peculiar, quavering, far-carrying call, as she came in with rats and gophers, field mice and moles, sent both her kittens and me racing pell-mell in her direction. Having the longest legs, I got there first.

That autumn, when I returned to home and school, I carried the catch of the season with me. It consisted mostly of mouse-skins and the whole bundle could be held in one hand. That, I had to admit, was a far cry from the great bundles of furs I had seen pictured on sleds coming out of the northern wilderness. But, nevertheless, it was a bundle of furs—no matter how small.

One Saturday morning, late that autumn, my pelts went to market. There were no Hudson Bay trading posts, with knives and guns and calico, on the busy streets of Joliet. There were only stores with plate-glass windows and efficiently arranged counters. Toward one of these establishments I headed—without divulging my intentions to anyone. I had noticed in the previous evening's issue of *The Joliet Herald* a large advertisement of a fur sale. The store selling the most furs, I reasoned, would be the place quickest in need of a new supply.

Somewhat timidly I climbed the stairs to the fur department. Under bright lights, which gleamed on the polished wood and glass of the showcases, fashionably dressed ladies were viewing themselves in full-length mirrors. Clerks hovered about them, admiring audibly the effect of each new fur-piece. Over all hung the depressing odor of moth-balls.

For a long time nobody paid any attention to me, an eight-year-old shifting from one foot to the other on the thick green carpet. Finally the manager of the department spied me. He walked briskly up. A little dubiously, he inquired:

"Like to look at some furs, young man?"

"I have some furs to sell."

"What kind of furs?"

"They are small furs."

"Well, where are they?"

He looked around and apparently saw nothing.

"They are here."

I tugged at the little bundle and it came out of my pocket with a jerk. The mouse pelts seemed to have shrunk in size. They suddenly appeared insignificant, almost microscopic.

The manager gave a start. Then he turned his back, seemingly to view in a better light the bundle of skins I had given him. For a moment he appeared overcome by an attack of ague. Then he got himself in hand and said:

"I must show these to the owner of the store. He has to decide on such purchases, you know."

He disappeared in an office and hastily closed the door. From inside came suppressed exclamations and stifled gurgles. In a few minutes the door opened a crack and the manager's hand beckoned to the head saleslady. She disappeared in the office and the door quickly clicked shut. Feminine giggles were added to the subdued sounds in the office.

The door then opened and out popped the head of a gray-haired man I had not seen before. He, I thought, must be the store owner. He stared at me, his face screwed up under the stress of obvious self-control. Then the head popped in and the door went shut.

A couple of minutes passed. Then out marched the head saleslady, her upper teeth showing in a reddened face as she bit her underlip. Behind came the fur-department manager. His face was also pink from pent-up emotion. He explained courteously that the store had all the furs it could use for the time being.

"While we can't make use of your furs ourselves," he

concluded, "I understand the Boston Store needs some. Ask for Mr. Bryant over there. And say I sent you."

While this advice was being offered, the head saleslady was whispering to a knot of clerks and customers beside one of the full-length mirrors. I felt all eyes were on me as I headed for the stairs. Just as I reached the top step, a heavy, florid woman, who had been trying on a silver-fox neckpiece, reached the limit of her self-control. She burst like a paper bag into a wheezing howl of laughter. A cackling uproar, like the alarm of a henyard when a hawk is sighted, broke out behind me as I hurried away down the stairs.

Several times I walked around the block before I built up sufficient courage to enter the Boston Store. Here, as soon as I approached the fur department, work ceased. A man with a carnation in his lapel hurried up with an air of pleasant anticipation. News of my coming evidently had preceded me.

No sooner had I pulled my little bundle of furs from my pocket than I was the center of a cluster of clerks, floorwalkers, and customers. One wanted to know how I trapped the animals. Another inquired what kind of bait I used. A third asked how I cured the pelts. At the end of ten minutes the questions petered out and I broached the subject of a purchase price. The cluster dissolved suddenly.

"I'll tell you what," said the man with the carnation. "We *were* in need of furs last week. But a new shipment came in. However, I believe they need furs badly over at

Ducker's Department Store. Mr. Johnson is the man to see. Be sure to tell him I sent you!"

My suspicions were justified when I entered the front door at Ducker's. As soon as I asked for Mr. Johnson, snickers followed me down the aisle. With a certain stubborn trait of character, I marched on. Mr. Johnson greeted me effusively. Before I could say a word, he exclaimed:

"Ah! So you are the young man with the pelts. Mr. Bryant phoned me you were coming."

I saw work cease and clerks begin converging toward us.

"Let's examine your furs," Mr. Johnson began, beaming and rubbing his hands together.

"I guess they aren't really furs," I blurted out. "They're only mouse-skins!"

Then I fled precipitately.

·6·

MONEY MATTERS

THE pig rode in state up to the farmhouse door. It was a small white pig and it was mine. Six months had elapsed since the episode of the mouse pelts. My parents, seeking to direct me into more normal activity, had engineered the purchase of the pig. They expected it would provide me with a never-to-be-forgotten object lesson in the value of thrift. It was to initiate me into the virtues and mysteries of compound interest.

"It," my mother had explained, "is a mamma pig. After a while it will have baby pigs. Some of them will be mamma pigs. They will have baby pigs. Starting with one pig, some day you may have a whole field full of pigs!"

In a way, the white pig had as its immediate ancestor a brown glazed china pig with a slot in its back. Through this slot I had been instructed to drop pennies and nickels and dimes during the winter before. The china pig was kept out of reach on the top of a cupboard and, from time to time, I was permitted to feel its increasing weight and to rattle the coins inside. When its contents passed the five-dollar mark, all the coins were taken out with the aid of a silver knife, which guided them through the slot, and given to Gramp for the purchase of a suitable mother pig.

I rode with him to a farm, three-quarters of a mile away. There he picked out the pig he wanted and stated he could pay five dollars for it but not a cent more. The owner of the farm was known to be "a little on the sharp side," but he had good pigs. He was an undersized man with a long nose and one weak eye which he kept partially closed as though he were continually sighting along a gun-barrel. He sniffed when he talked. As Gramp said, he was "a hemmer and a hawer."

He remained silent a long time after he heard Gramp's terms. Before venturing to speak, he cleared his throat.

"I, er"—sniff—"I, ah"—sniff. Then he fell silent, sighting up at a treetop. Minutes passed. He cleared his throat again.

"Well, Ed"—sniff—"I, ah . . ." His voice trailed off. In silence he followed the flight of a swallow circling his big red barn. He cleared his throat and we waited expectantly. Instead of speaking, he stood on one leg and swished a heavy-soled shoe back and forth through the grass, sending up a small cloud of dust and pollen. Fully five minutes had gone by before he came to the great decision.

"Thet pig, y'know, Ed"—sniff—"is a mighty likely young sow"—long pause and a final sniff—"but y' kin have 'er fer the five dollars ef the boy wants 'er."

We loaded the white pig in a special crate we had brought in the cracker-wagon and started for home. At the kitchen door Gram came out to see the animal.

"What are you going to name her, Edwin?" she wanted to know after she had shaded her eyes and peered between the slats of the crate. I hadn't thought of that. Finally we decided on the name "Flora."

Flora was to live in the same pen with Gramp's young pigs. I was to pay for her board and keep by carrying one pail of swill a day to dump in the hog-trough. Once Flora had been deposited safely within the fenced-in enclosure, I felt I was in business. I was launched on a sea of compound interest.

That term, compound interest, was not unknown to me even before the advent of the white pig. For it played a prominent part in a Lone Oak joke of long standing.

In the year 1872 Gramp had promised to take Gram to a Fourth of July celebration at Michigan City. A few years before, the vanguard of the Colorado potato beetles, advancing eastward from the Rockies at the rate of about eighty-five miles a year, had reached Indiana. In 1872 a wave of these agricultural pests enveloped the potato field at Lone Oak. Fourth of July came and Gramp shook his head gravely.

" 'Mimy," he said, "I guess we better pick beetles instead o' goin' t' th' celebration. Ef y' help git those pesky bugs off th' vines, I'll tell y' what I'll do. I'll give y' one-third o' all th' cash th' crop brings in."

Gram agreed and all that Fourth of July she knocked beetles off into a tin pail half-filled with kerosene. Fall came and her share of the potato crop amounted to $24.00. But there was illness that year and sudden expenses. They decided to wait until the next harvest season to pay the amount. And so it went, from year to year. An annual hilarious rite, at the time I was small, occurred when the daughters of the family were all home for some holiday. With pencils and papers they would figure up, at six per cent compound interest, what Gramp then owed Gram for the beetles she picked. By the summer of the white pig, the amount had pyramided to $253.22—more than ten and a half times the original sum.

Gramp, on these occasions, would chuckle and say:

"Won't be long now afore we'll have t' sell th' whole farm t' pay Mother her bug-money!"

"Right now," he once added, "I couldn't buy a shingle ef th' whole meetin' house was fer sale fer a cent!"

Another time he observed: "Maybe it's no disgrace t' be poor—but it's mighty inconvenient!"

Of course, Gramp wasn't poor, any more than he was rich. He had money in the bank; he owned his farm; he had put his children through college. But excess cash was never plentiful. Although hunger and want were unknown, luxuries were few and far between. And, in the early days, he and Gram had had to scrimp to make ends meet. Gramp's gold watch, the heavy timepiece he had carried through the Civil War, was a friend in need during many financial crises before the farm was paid for. Half a dozen times Gramp parted company with it, leaving it as security for a loan—to be reclaimed at harvest time.

The big financial hurdle of the year, tax-time, came as regularly as groundhog day. And it always found Gramp unprepared. Easy-going and full of jokes during the rest of the year, he would suddenly settle down to the serious business of raising cash. There would be a hurrying and scurrying, an attempt to sell everything in sight. After this storm, calm would reign again.

Acquisitiveness was not an important element in the character of either my grandfather or my grandmother. Gramp was too kindly disposed to drive a hard bargain and Gram was too impulsively generous, too sure that the real wealth of the world lay in books and learning.

Once, in her early married life when all the ready money Gram possessed was a silver dollar hidden in a wooden wall-clock, an elderly stranger knocked at the front door. He told a pitiful tale of want that brought tears to Gram's eyes. When he left, the silver dollar was in his pocket. Unfortunately, when he stopped at a neighboring farmhouse and told of "the good lady down the road" who had given him a whole dollar, he was recognized as an impostor from Burdick. The neighbors hailed Gramp as he drove past that evening, on his way home from town:

"Ed, y' must hev money t' burn down t' yer place! 'Mimy give a whole dollar t' an old snide from Burdick while y' was t' town."

Another year one of the other neighbors, tired of hearing how well-read Gram was and how many books she owned, decided to own a book, too. Her choice was a popular novel, selling for a dollar and a half. After she had read it, she stopped at Lone Oak.

"I don't have any more use fer th' book," she explained to Gram. "Thought y' might want t' buy it. I can't *afford* t' keep good money tied up in *books*. Noticed *you* never seemed t' mind, though."

Gram didn't buy it. But she did continue to buy the books and magazines she wanted whenever the opportunity offered. It was a luxury she permitted herself even though the opinion of the community was virtually unanimous that it was an act of wanton and willful extravagance.

Although, at Lone Oak, they worried about the taxes, Gramp and Gram were singularly independent. They were servants to none. They steered by their own stars. Although they had known want, as pioneers knew it, they had nothing but contempt for anyone who married for money. They knew the freedom of sincerity. They had no false front to maintain. They had no desire to fool or mislead, no wish to impress people that they were greater than they were.

At one end of a long room at the Metropolitan Museum of Art, in New York City, a celebrated painting by Jules Bastien-Lepage shows the maid of Orleans, Joan of Arc, standing in her humble farm dooryard at Domremy. The simplicity and sincerity of her surroundings have been caught by the brush of the painter. In the loneliness of my first year in the great city I often sought out this picture. That country dooryard of a distant land was, in many ways, like the one I remembered so well at Lone Oak. Both were, to use the Wordsworth phrase, the scenes of simple living and high thinking. Honesty and high ideals inhabited them both.

I valued these latter virtues all the more as the unexpected consequence of my contact with compound interest in the form of little pigs. The results of that initial business venture were far from those expected.

On the morning after Flora came to our farm, I rushed out to see if there were any baby pigs in the pen. There wasn't even Flora!

"Maybe she's all covered with mud so y' don't recognize her," Gramp consoled me when I arrived breathless back at the house.

But such was not the case. Gramp poked in the shed and routed out all the pigs. Flora was not among them. Then he circled the pen, examining the fence minutely. At the far side, where the bottom-board of the fence was nailed to a soft sassafras post, the pig had pushed her way to freedom. Gramp got an ear of corn and walked about the barnyard calling:

"Here, Pooey! Pooey! Pooey!"

But no Flora appeared. He put down the corn and began to follow the tracks left by the small cloven hoofs. They headed straight for the farm where we had bought the pig. After breakfast we hitched Dolly to the buggy and drove up to see the owner.

"I dunno," Gramp ruminated as we rolled along, "whether he'll admit it even ef th' pig did come home."

He probably was recalling an event at the last election. So intent was the pig-raiser on getting the best of his fellow-men that he practiced up on unimportant trifles. As Gramp was leaving the voting-place, the man had hailed him:

"Who'd y' vote fer, Ed?" he asked with only a minor sniff.

"I voted fer George Martin. Who'd y' vote fer?"

"That's fer me t' know"—sniff—"an' fer y' t' find out!"

With that he had ambled off chuckling to himself.

As we turned up his driveway, the farmer was coming from the pig-yard. Gramp asked him if he had seen the white pig we had bought the day before, explaining what had happened. After a minute or two of rumination, while he sighted away across a lower pasture, he observed:

"Well, ah, y'know, Ed, that'd be putty hard t' tell. Lota pigs"—sniff—"in my pen."

"Did y' see a little white pig outside th' pen this morning?"

After a long delay, he cleared his throat.

"Yes I did, Ed," he admitted. "But"—sniff—"there were five o' my young pigs outa the pen. Mighta been one o' them, y'know. Got outa hole. Don't see how we can be sure."

He sighted at Gramp for a sharp instant, then squinted up into the branches of an elm tree. Gramp climbed into his buggy. We hadn't marked Flora. We had no sure means of identification.

"Th' old *cundermudgeon!*" Gramp muttered as we drove back to the farm. "He knows blasted well that's your pig."

Suddenly I was struck by a thought. Flora was gone and so were the little compound-interest piglets that were to lead to a whole field of pigs. Not only that but *where was my five dollars?* Long and loud I began to bewail my misfortune.

"Never you mind," Gram consoled me when we reached home. "We'll see that you get *that* money back anyhow."

Later my father made up the loss. But he was unable to restore my faith in the wonders and infallible riches which lay like a pot of gold at the end of the rainbow of compound interest. The object-lesson had miscarried. Flora might have stood as a symbol for the dangers of speculation, but she provided but a poor example of the rewards of sound investment.

·7·

THE WHEELY-CART

SMARTWEED grew between the spokes of the discarded carriage wheels. There were four of them and they lay in a heap in a far corner of the woodyard. Each was almost as high as my head.

As I looked at the weathered wheels, a plan took shape in my mind. When I was five I had gravely explained to Gram my idea for a "wheely-cart." It was to run on railroad tracks like a train. But when it met another train head-on it was to lift into the air on wings, sail along, and then settle down on the tracks beyond. Thus wheely-cart trains could run in both directions on the same tracks.

Now, as I gazed at the abandoned wheels, I decided to put my idea into practice, to build a real wheely-cart—or at least to take a step in that direction.

Heaving the wheels upright out of the tangle of weeds, I rolled them to a fence and propped them up. Then I went in search of Verne Bradfield. Verne was a boy of about my age who had moved into the house across the road and to the east of Lone Oak. Slender and sandy-haired, he spoke with a drawl and possessed a keen imagination. The circumstances of our first memorable meeting will be told later.

Verne and I set to work amid the chips of the woodyard. We whittled down the ends of sassafras poles until they were the right diameter to fit in the hubs of the wheels. Then we smeared black axle-grease on the whittled portions, slipped on the wheels, and anchored them in place by driving in ten-penny nails near the ends of the poles. This accomplished, we laid a plank across the two sassafras axles and secured it with more nails. The wheely-cart was finished. True, the wheels wobbled and the whole thing had the rickety appearance of a colt standing on its feet for the first time. But it rolled along when we pushed it.

Gramp came up from cultivating and looked at the wheely-cart in amazement. He said:

"What won't a feller see when he ain't got his gun!"

The career of the wheely-cart was short-lived. We decided to ride downhill and headed it away from the clothes-yard down the driveway. I straddled the plank and Verne gave a hard push. The wheely-cart gained momentum. It jolted along, bounced out of the driveway, and started across a sloping field of sand and clover. Then three wheels came off all at once. The sudden plunge snapped the two sassafras axles and left me sprawling in the sand. Together Verne and I lugged the various parts back to the woodyard and turned to other pursuits.

When Verne and I were together, other pursuits were always numerous. Shortly after we met, he had confided:

"Y' know, Edwin, I'm gun-crazy."

So, for a time, were we both. We used to whittle away for hours on pieces of soft white pine, shaping life-sized shotguns and rifles which we painted realistic colors. With such hunting weapons held ready, we would wander afield on the trail of imaginary deer and catamounts.

Once, while we were skirting the lower meadow, we came upon Gramp oiling his mowing-machine. His two work-horses—Deck, a big, white-footed, slow-moving horse, and Colty, an all-brown animal which Gramp had raised from a colt and called "Colty" all the rest of its life—were resting in the shade.

"Mr. Way," Verne inquired with great formality, "can y' tell us if there's any good huntin' in this neighborhood?"

"There certainly is!" Gramp assured him. "There's fine huntin' all 'round here. But," he added, "I don't know whether y'll find anythin' er not!"

He chuckled and we laughed out loud.

"Boys," he asked, "did I ever tell y' about Mr. Bump an' th' quail? No? Well, Mr. Bump was a great hunter. One time he came to a place where a lot o' quail were sittin' on top o' a zigzag rail fence. He wanted t' git 'em all, but th' only gun he had with him was a single-ball musket. He studied fer a long while. Then, y' know what he did? He bent th' barrel o' his gun zigzag jest like th' fence. When he fired, th' ball traveled zigzag an' killed ever' last quail all down th' length o' th' fence! He told me so, himself," Gramp added.

Not far from the Lone Oak spring, cattle had trampled a marshy spot into a pond a dozen feet across. On the shores of this miniature lake, Verne and I had two adventures. One early June day we were banging away at imaginary mallards and pintails when I looked down and saw, almost at our feet, a small black and white snake curled into a figure-eight. Of one accord we raced in a panic for the barnyard, our guns waving in the air as we ran.

Our second adventure occurred in late March, during one of my Easter vacations. A thaw had melted the ice on the pasture pool. In probing around in the pond with sticks, we unearthed a hibernating frog. It was buried in mud and, until we thawed it out, was as stiff as though frozen. Our amazement knew no bounds. For days thereafter we barraged Gramp and Gram with questions about how all the varied summer creatures spent the wintertime.

After a couple of years Verne's family moved to Sunbury, Ohio. Three decades passed before I saw him again. Not long after his disappearance, another boyhood companion moved into the farmhouse over the hill beyond the great oak tree. His name was Dewey Gunder. Slightly smaller, and a little younger, than I, he had brilliant blue eyes and an engaging smile. These two, Verne and Dewey, were my main boy-companions of the time. But, year in and year out, my closest chums were Gramp and Gram.

One Christmas vacation the night outside the Lone Oak farmhouse was filled with a volleying that made us sit up in our beds. Pioneer automobiles, starting from New York on a race around the world, were plowing through snow on the old sand road. The leaders reached Furnessville that night and stragglers passed our farm for days afterward. What happened to them after they disappeared beyond the western hill I never heard. But that floundering passage of the vanguard of the motor age turned our thoughts to engines and automobiles and motorcycles.

Dewey and I were bitten by the motor-bug as badly as Verne and I had been bitten by the gun-bug. We raced down to the gate to watch every passing car and oftentimes, holding forked sticks in front of us—to form the handlebars of imaginary motorcycles—we would go chugging and clucking about the fields in round-the-world races of our own. In the snow, after the passing of the automobile cavalcade, I had picked up a black leather gauntlet which one of the racers had lost. I wore it wherever I went. It was, I felt, a close link to all the vast movement of motored advance.

A glorious day that lived long in memory was one in

which a passing motorcyclist skidded into a ditch and damaged his shining new twin-cylinder Indian motorcycle. Unable to get it started, he hired Gramp to haul the machine in his lumber wagon back to Michigan City. All during the long drive I sat astride the motorcycle holding the rubber grip of one of the handlebars in my black-gauntleted hand.

For a long time, one summer, Dewey and I tried—without much success—to break a calf in as a riding pony. Then we turned our attention to a large and placid pig. The runway of the pigpen skirted the western side of the barnyard. Here we cornered the porker and I climbed on its broad, smooth back. Dewey slipped a binding-twine loop over its snout and passed back a length of the string for reins. The pig took all these indignities calmly. It seemed to have none of the fire of an Arabian steed in its makeup. It walked around in deliberate circles while my feet plowed little furrows in the dust as they dragged along the ground.

Dewey soon tired of this tame exhibition. He took off his wide-brimmed straw hat and slapped the pig smartly on the rump. The effect was almost magical. Instantly the porker rushed away, carrying me clinging to my binding-twine reins and struggling to keep my balance. Dewey whooped behind.

The ride ended as suddenly as it began. While I was pulling myself upright after nearly losing my hold, the pig scuttled under the projecting end of the upper pole of the barnyard bars. The pole was just on a level with my forehead. It swept me off the animal's back as though I had been a fly. Trailing its binding-twine halter, the pig disappeared into its shed and left me lying flat on my back with shooting stars and a black and whirling world before my eyes.

Another adventure, in which Dewey shared, contributed to my out-of-doors education. We were returning home down one of the brush-lined paths of the north woods near twilight when I thought I sighted a lost kitten on the trail ahead of us. It seemed unafraid, innocent, and furry. Neither one of us was quite sure what the creature was, although we both probably had our suspicions. It seemed so charming, so attractive, so disarming that I whispered to Dewey to head it off.

While he floundered through the underbrush, our intended quarry trotted ahead of me without accelerating its pace. It had an air of knowing more than I did. Dewey appeared in the path ahead. I closed in. But my outstretched hand never reached the furry body it was aiming at. The little animal's tail flipped up. That was the last I saw. Gasping for breath, I was enveloped in a cloud of choking gas, rising from blinding liquid sprayed at close range.

Dewey and I agreed later that being a skunk under such circumstances must be a lot of fun.

My homecoming that evening was anything but a triumphal entry. The breeze was from the north and my approach was heralded from afar. Dewey rushed off, suddenly remembering his chores. Gram indignantly shooed me away from the kitchen door. She handed out clean clothes on the end of a broom and tossed me a cake of Ivory soap. When I appeared at the barn door, where Gramp was milking, he shouted: "Jumpin' Jehosephat!"

"Skedaddle out o' here," he commanded, "or y'll curdle th' milk!"

Disconsolately, I wandered to the lower end of the barnyard, buried my overalls in sand, and lathered beside the pasture pool. In spite of many sudsings, my hair retained more or less faint remnants of the wood-pussy's perfume for weeks afterward.

"I suppose," Gram observed as she ladled hot mush into my bowl that night, "I suppose you've got to learn. But I wish you'd do it on somebody else's farm!"

·8·

RIB-WALKERS

THERE were, in those days, other forms of life which—even more than the birds, the animals, the insects—occupied my mind. They were those crawling creatures that "walk on their ribs," the serpent inhabitants of the dune country.

Because of its swamps and hills and wide stretches of wasteland, the region provided these rib-walkers with an ideal home. The area was good "snake country." However, Gramp assured me that the reptiles of my day were but frail and ghostly descendants of the great snakes he had encountered when he came west as a boy. Both in size and number they had dwindled sadly away.

"In those days," he told me, "I often put up a cord o' snakes before breakfast. And it didn't have t' be good snake weather, either!"

To the north of us, beyond the trees of the Lone Oak woods, there lay a wide sandy tract, untouched by the plow and given over to mullein and sandburrs. It was a veritable field of the serpents. Its long abandonment by man and the numerous tunnels of the gophers, field mice, and moles made it a sort of reptile paradise.

Verne and I were attracted irresistibly to the area. We used to stare with mingled horror and fascination at the snake-tracks winding and crisscrossing on the open sand. Here was a sort of Garden of Eden in reverse. The serpents were living in their paradise and man was the interloper.

Most of this reptilian population consisted of harmless garter snakes, blue racers, and blacksnakes. Beyond, where the sandy tract dipped down to an extensive stretch of lowland, a marsh spread out its tangled expanse as a special chamber of horrors. There, we had been told, dwelt the dreaded masassauga, or prairie rattlesnake.

One day, as we stood looking into the thick vegetation of this swamp—where in our heated imagination every tussock sheltered what Gramp called a "snaddledrake"—Verne gave voice to a sentiment which impressed me greatly at the time.

"Ef one o' them there rattlers bit me," he declared, "know what I'd do? I'd foller him right into that swamp.

I wouldn't be scairt o' nothin'. I wouldn't stop 'til I'd stomped the life out o' him!"

Near the eastern boundary of Lone Oak another spot was closely associated with a giant among the rib-walkers. At this place an immense maple tree lifted its symmetrical form above a clump of low bushes. Cattle sought its shade at noontime and their stamping feet had exposed a portion of the buried mat of interlacing roots. A black hole, with no dirt around its opening, descended mysteriously among these roots.

One summer Gramp came to the house from mowing in the lower forty. He had sighted "the biggest snake you ever saw" near the giant maple. While he was hunting a stick, the reptile had disappeared among the bushes at the base of the tree. The following year Gramp saw the snake again, and again it vanished as before. The big serpent became an elusive, almost legendary reptile.

Verne and I hunted over the region, stepping high and stopping in every open space to look around, with clubs poised for ready use. Moving through the grass, we swished our sticks back and forth. We made all the noise we could—like a man descending the stairs to see if there are burglars in the house.

Twice we sighted the big reptile. It seemed at least twenty feet long as its sinuous black body slid swiftly toward the maple tree. On our second encounter we were close enough to see it reach the mat of exposed roots. Its long body quickly poured itself into the hole and disappeared. We poked in our sticks with no result. That afternoon we returned with a steel muskrat trap. Setting it carefully at the entrance to the burrow, we went away.

Early the next morning we returned. The great blacksnake was dead. Its head was caught in the jaws of the trap; its long, glistening body stretched away, limp and lifeless, among the exposed roots of the maple tree. In triumph we carried our prize to Gramp. With his folding pocket-rule, he measured the snake. It had a total length of more than seven feet. It was an old-timer and, in later days, we referred to it as the King of the Blacksnakes.

Among the innumerable snake-stories which I heard or read at that time the one which remains most vivid in my mind appeared in the local weekly newspaper. During the early-autumn weeks the story ran on for several issues.

In the hill country of eastern Kentucky, the first dispatch reported, a gigantic serpent had been carrying off sheep and calves. No one had seen the reptile. But its trail, half as wide as a wagon-road, had been followed where it dragged its great coils across the countryside. A follow-up story told how, on another foray, the Kentucky serpent had pulled its length across a stone fence, leaving behind scattered boulders and a wide gap where it had made its passage.

The final installment of the story related the adventures of a party of daring hunters. They had followed the trail of the serpent far back into the mountains. In a wild chasm, strewn with dead and fallen trees, the track of the gigantic reptile led straight to the mouth of a forbidding cavern. The hunters had hurriedly blocked up the entrance of the cave with large boulders and then had hastened away down the mountainside. Heavy snows had fallen shortly afterward. The following spring, the newspaper item declared, the men intended to return, open the cavern, and dispatch the giant reptile.

Accepting the story as gospel truth, I awaited impatiently for the spring. I scanned each issue of the paper as soon as it arrived by mail. But no conclusion to the tale appeared. The editor, with the cunning of his craft, nimbly skipped to other matters and, so far as I know, no embarrassing questions about this super-serpent ever came from his readers.

Even the person who is normally truthful finds difficulty in speaking truthfully about encounters with snakes. I recall an early instance which has returned innumerable times to memory.

In my twelfth summer Gramp let me handle a team and plow alone for the first time. He turned me loose in a long field which bordered the marsh and the "island." Here there were no stumps or stones to snag and the plowing was relatively simple. The polished share sliced through the black loam of the bottomlands, turning a crinkled ribbon of damp glistening soil to the right as we worked down the long field.

Suddenly I caught a momentary flash of a snake, plowed unharmed from the ground, rising from the soil toward me. It struck my body then wriggled rapidly away —a common, harmless garter snake. That noon, when I drove the team up to the farmhouse, I was bursting with my great adventure.

"I plowed up a snake and it hit me clear up on my chest!" I told Gram.

"Are you sure? That seems awful high to me."

"Uh-huh. I *know* it hit me on the chest!"

"Well, Edwin, if you say so, I'm bound to believe you. But," she added, "if it was anybody else, I'd have my doubts."

At the time I was sure. I could see it in my own mind as plain as day. Yet, all the while, something in the back of my consciousness told me it wasn't true. And now I know, by all the laws of probability and physics, that the reptile could not have brushed against my legs higher than my knees.

Haying time at Lone Oak was the season of the year when my dread of snakes reached its peak. For all the small dwellers in a field of timothy, what a time of terror and disaster haying must bring! How suddenly its blitzkrieg must lay waste their homeland! The mouse, the toad, the frog, the meadowlark, the garter snake, all see their familiar world dissolve in wreckage around them. The shuttling knives of the mower, the bouncing steel teeth of the rake, the sharp, gleaming tines of the pitchfork, the rumbling juggernaut of the hay-wagon, all leave behind them death and destruction.

I could, perhaps, sympathize more clearly with these small creatures because for me, too, haying-time was a time of apprehension and dread. On top of the load, I would see Gramp heave the great forkfuls of hay upward from the floor of the field. As each forkful soared rapidly closer I would imagine a reptile was riding toward me entangled in the hay.

Nor was this fear entirely groundless. There was one nightmare moment on a windy day in July. We had begun to bring in the marsh hay from beside the Père Marquette tracks that morning. Two loads had already gone into the mow and the third load was nearly completed. High aloft, I was tramping down the front of the load when Gramp came to the last cock in the row.

I saw him throw his weight on the handle, driving the tines deep into the conical mass of hay. Then he gave a sudden upward heave and the mass loomed closer. Struggling with it in the wind, he landed it close beside me and pulled the fork away. I trampled it into place. Then I glanced out to where Gramp was walking on to the next row, his fork slung over his shoulder. A triphammer blow seemed to strike me in the pit of the stomach; all the blood in my body drained away in one moment of terror.

In thrusting his fork into the last cock, Gramp had driven one of the tines through the thick body of a rattlesnake. It now writhed and lashed about just beyond reach of his shoulders. My voice came back and I screeched a shrill warning. The wind carried my words away. Again and again I screamed at the top of my voice. Gramp walked on without hearing my calls.

The age-long seconds which followed had a nightmare quality about them—the boy screaming from the high-piled load of hay, the man walking calmly over the field, the impaled rattler lashing this way and that. Finally Gramp sensed that the vibrations in the fork-handle were not the work of the wind. He glanced around. What he saw turned him to swift and decisive action.

When the rattler was dead, I scrambled down from the load. Watching my step, and mindful of the old adage that rattlers always go in twos, I approached and gazed on the formidable body. Gramp went calmly on with his work. As for me, that experience returned, magnified and embellished, in snake nightmares which haunted me in ensuing years.

My dread of snakes was abnormal. It was more than physical fear. In my mind these dread creatures seemed to possess supernatural powers, to lead a charmed life, to be immune to the laws which governed other living things. The amazement which I felt when I killed my first rattler, and discovered how easily it met its death, remains a vivid memory.

I was raking hay in a lower field when I caught the sharp rattle of the serpent. For an instant I saw it. Then it disappeared as though the ground had swallowed it up —which in truth, it had. Gramp brought a shovel and I stood ready with a long-handled post-hole digger. With his first thrust of the spade, Gramp uncovered the burrow in which the snake had taken refuge. Out it came, tail vibrating and flat head raised.

Gramp struck at it with the spade and missed. The serpent coiled. Swinging the post-hole digger as though I were slaying a bullock, I crashed it down on the coiled reptile. Gramp gave a screech of dismay as he foresaw the fate of his post-hole digger. There was a splintering crash. The oak handle had snapped in two from the force of the blow. I had expected a desperate struggle, many blows, in dispatching so formidable an enemy. I stared in amazement. One blow, a small fraction as great as the one I had delivered, would have ended the life of even the largest diamondback.

I would like to say that in that moment of realization of the essential frailty of this great enemy of mine my fears vanished forever. But this was not true. The haunted visions of early years had worn too deep a trail across my mind to be erased in a single day. Decades of gradual change effected a return to reason. But, even today, when I can view a snake in the open without alarm, a harmless serpent weaving through grass and weeds stirs to life an emotion of panic which is the heritage of bygone days.

"We all know," wrote the French philosopher, Blaise Pascal, "that the sight of a reptile . . . will at times utterly overpower a man's reason. Place the profoundest philosopher that ever lived on a plank even wider than need be, and if there be a precipice below, while reason proves his safety, imagination will prevail."

Many years after the experiences related in this chapter I spent a day with Dr. Raymond L. Ditmars at his reptile house in the Bronx Zoo. I watched him milk the venom from cottonmouths and diamondbacks. I saw him handling cobras and copperheads. By understanding their natures, and by applying his knowledge, he was master of a huge collection of varied reptiles.

I left him late in the afternoon, after mustering up courage to handle a harmless snake myself. I felt that my early fears were finally gone. My mind henceforth would be master of my old emotions. Then, as I was making my way out in the dim light of a corridor behind the serpent cages, I stepped on a length of rubber hose. The catamount screech and the gazelle-leap that followed were automatic. Like Pascal's philosopher, my mind had been convinced but my imagination still prevailed.

·9·

STRAWBERRY TRAIN

DAWN-MIST lay on the lowlands. The clean, sweet smell of the morning fields filled the air. And all across the wide strawberry patch dew-drops edged the heart-shaped leaves and glinted in the rising sun. Gramp and I had begun picking at five o'clock in the morning. Gray smoke, trailing upward from the kitchen chimney, told us that Gram was cooking breakfast.

Strawberries, together with asparagus, brought in the earliest revenue of the season at Lone Oak. Then, about the Fourth of July, came the early rose potatoes. They were followed by the red Astrakhan apples and the grain harvest. Finally came the fall crops, the pumpkins, corn, turnips, squash, late potatoes and autumn apples. Each June Gramp shipped hundreds of crates of strawberries to the market in Chicago.

As I worked down my first row, moving ahead on hands and knees that soon were dripping with dew, I remembered the beginning of that favorite of my childhood books, Charles Kingsley's *The Water Babies.* So many times had I read it, and had it read to me, that I could quote pages on end from memory. Now I recalled the dawn-scene in the first chapter when all the strange adventures began for Tom, the little chimney-sweep, and Grimes, his master; when they set out for the great country estate and:

"Grimes rode the donkey in front, and Tom and the brushes walked behind—out of the court, and up the street, past the closed window-shutters, and the winking weary policemen, and the roofs all shining gray in the gray dawn. They passed through the pitmen's village . . . and then they were out in the real country. The road grew white, and the walls likewise; and at the wall's foot grew long grass and gay flowers, all drenched with dew; and instead of the groaning of the pit-engine, they heard the skylark saying his matins high up in the air, and the pit-bird warbling in the sedges."

Around us, too, as we filled the thin-walled wooden boxes with red berries, the dawn chorus of the birds rose from fence and tree and bush. Before breakfast we had picked nearly a crate between us. From then until late afternoon, the picking went on at top speed. Gram helped us. A Polish family from across the lowland marsh arrived with a troop of children to aid in the berry harvest. Gramp nailed up the cases as they were filled and placed them in the shade. We all carried four or eight boxes in handled wooden carriers and when we delivered them filled to Gramp we received little colored slips of cardboard—red and blue and yellow—marked "4 QUARTS," "8 QUARTS," or "16 QUARTS." These slips, about an inch and a half by an inch in size, formed the currency of the strawberry fields. Later they could be transformed into coin of the realm, the rate of payment being a cent and a half a quart—or, late in the season when berries grew scarce, two cents a quart.

As the sun climbed higher and the heat increased, my trips to the cellar pump became more frequent. Sometimes Gram would bring out a quart Mason jar in a pail of cold spring water. The jar would be filled with homemade ginger ale or root beer, a beverage which brought to mind woodland tastes—of sassafras twig-tips and wintergreen berries. But even with these aids the chore grew more and more tiresome.

I remember one afternoon when the largest of the Polish boys, a hulking boy-man of fifteen, stood up suddenly and said in a loud voice to his mother picking beside him: "I won't pick!"

Without saying a word, his mother swung her right arm

in a sweeping arc. The slap resounded across the strawberry patch. The boy said: "I will pick!" and bent to his task again.

As the afternoon advanced, Gramp would try to spur us on. The "Strawberry Express" left Furnessville, a mile and a half away on the Michigan Central Railroad, at five-thirty. From two o'clock onward he would say at intervals:

"'S'bout train time. Better hurry up!"

From four o'clock on the pressure increased. The horses stood waiting, hitched to the light cracker-wagon. Crates were loaded in; the final quarts came hurrying in from the field; the last crate-cover was nailed in place and the last rubber stamp slammed down on the final crate before it took its place on top of the others. Then Gramp and I would jump into the driver's seat, Gramp would look at his big gold watch for a final time and away we would go in a cloud of dust. The picking was over for the day.

But the main excitement was only beginning. It was this race against time to which I had looked forward during the dreariest part of the day. Gramp, in common with the other strawberry-raisers of the region, had the trip to the station timed to the second. Up Bert's hill, down and across the tracks, past Asa Colgrove's and Jim Forbes' and Lewrey's store. By now the distant whistle of the train would be sounding for Smith's crossing, behind us. The last eighth of a mile was made with sound and fury in billowing clouds of dust. It was like the chariot race in *Ben Hur*. As we pulled up with horses snorting and covered with sweat, other wagons were piling into the narrow confines of the station yard. The train slowed. With spurting puffs of white steam, it ground to a stop.

For the next ten minutes all was confusion. Nat, the local station-agent, rushed from pile to pile, making out express bills for the shipments. He hopped about, the personification of excitement. His excitability was a synonym in the region. Every time a train came in, even if only one passenger got aboard, he bustled about as though he had more to do than he could handle. With the flood of strawberries descending on him at the last minute, he was almost beside himself. Trainmen shouted for him to hurry and local inhabitants drooped themselves over the station-fence to watch the fun.

Eventually all the crates had disappeared into the doorways of the express cars and the "Strawberry Special," with its single passenger car at the back, puffed off down the tracks toward Porter. The effect was something like that of the falling sky-rocket—what had started in shooting clouds of fire descended a burned-out stick. So the excitement suddenly went out of the station-yard with the departure of the train. Onlookers left the fence and strolled toward home. Farmers climbed into their wagons and turned the heads of their horses out into the sand-road. Nat, with a final warning—repeated from the day before and the day before that—that he would *not* accept any crates that didn't arrive well before traintime, wiped his streaming brow and disappeared through the doorway of his green-and-white station—a tiny structure with a dark interior which exhaled the odor of kerosene lamps and stale tobacco smoke and which resounded to the metallic and mysterious sound of the clicking telegraph.

Nat had been station-master for nearly thirty years. A short man, he habitually wore roomy clothes which often made him look as wide as he was high. His gray beard spread out over his chest as he walked along with head bent and his hands clasped behind him. Years later, when he was nearing retirement age, the station at Furnessville was closed because of dwindling patronage and Nat was given a job tending a crossing in a near-by city until his pension-age arrived.

Here his excitable nature flourished in fertile ground. He used to lean from his tower, almost tumbling to the ground, as he shouted and gesticulated to reckless motorists who sped across the tracks as the gates descended. The crossing soon became one of the show-places of the town and when Nat was pensioned he was greatly missed.

In his early years Nat had fallen in love with a farmer's daughter and was engaged to be married. Before the date of the ceremony an itinerant evangelist stopped at the village. The religious fervor of one of the meetings was so intense it affected the nerves of the young girl. Throughout the rest of her life she was subject to fits of nervous disorder. Nat said he had promised to marry her and he would. For forty years and more he provided her with the best he could afford, faithful to his ideal of conduct.

As express-trains thundered through the deserted village where the unused station stood, during the latter years of Nat's life, conductors used to throw off daily papers at his dooryard as a mark of respect. His heart bothered him a good deal during his last years. He used to walk slowly, like Conrad's Ransome, not daring to wake the wrath of this mortal enemy it was his bad fortune to carry within his breast. Yet each night he would walk slowly across the tracks to a neighboring farmhouse and return with a quart of fresh milk. This was the one luxury he permitted himself out of his small pension. The milk provided a nightly feast for a horde of half-wild cats that lived under his woodpile.

After the excitement of delivering the strawberries was over, Gramp and I would ride slowly back down the sand-road in the direction of Lone Oak. At Lewrey's store we would pull up and tie Deck and Colty to the iron pipe which ran through four heavy posts. Then we would enter the cavernous interior. Crossing the threshold was like entering some Valhalla of the sense of smell. Our nostrils were assailed by a thousand and one odors mingling together—the mysterious smell of spice and coffee, commodities from tropical lands, of coal oil and sugar and cheese and crackers and vinegar and overalls and rubber boots. Saws and axes hung in a corner and shelves held everything from bolts of calico to lamp-chimneys packed in excelsior.

All these items of exchange meant nothing to me. My rapt attention rarely wandered from the rows of glass jars which reproduced the rainbow in confection form. While Gramp bought himself a package of long-cut and filled his pipe with the slow deliberation of a man whose main work for the day was over, I deliberated between the various jars of stick candy—between the barber-pole design of the peppermint sticks, the pale yellow of the lemon, the bright red of the cinnamon, the black of the licorice, and the pale-green of the lime.

My decision reached, my purchases made, we climbed once more into the wagon and let the tired horses set their own pace toward the farmhouse gate. Gramp puffed contentedly on his pipe and I sampled each of my candy-flavors in turn. In the soft June dusk we rode on, at peace with the world. Ahead, on the following day, lay further excitement—the excitement of catching another strawberry train.

·10·

HOOPSNAKES

DURING the strawberry season, when my back began to ache with stooping, I used to relieve the monotony by begging Gram to tell—for the hundredth time—how she saw the hoopsnake.

Her memory of that event improved with the years and each re-telling of the story brought forth some fresh, corroborative detail. I would exclaim in delight:

"You never told me *that* before!"

And Gram would answer in all sincerity:

"I just remembered it. It comes back now as clear as day."

The story always started out the same and I desired no other beginning.

"It was in the early days," Gram would say, "long before you were born. Deer lived here then and a few remaining Indians. Father had planted his first strawberry patch on the slope near the spring."

"The same spring we have now?" I would ask, seeking to stretch out the story.

"Yes, the very same spring. A hayfield ran along the eastern edge of the berry patch. Well, one June day we were picking berries there. I remember I had a tin pail full and was just straightening up when I saw the snake."

"Was it really rolling along like a wheel?"

"No, it was crawling along like any other snake when I first saw it. It was blackish and about six feet long. It was coming straight for us. As I stood up, it saw me and turned toward the hayfield. It ran along the edge, just inside the grass, and as it went its head kept rising higher and higher, and just below where the pasture fence is now it grabbed its tail in its mouth and rolled away like a hoop out of sight. I was so excited, I remember, I tipped over the whole pail of berries and had to pick them up again."

"Did you see it too, Gramp?" I always wanted to know.

"Well, kind uv," he would reply judiciously. "But Mother saw 't best."

I used to query Gramp in private about that "kind uv." But all he would volunteer was: "Yer gran-maw wouldn't tell a lie. Ef she says she saw 't roll, she prob'ly did—at least, I'm sartin she thinks she did."

Gram was not the only one in the dune country ready to swear to a first-hand glimpse of a hoopsnake. These legendary rolling reptiles were commonplace in the folklore of the time and the region. Wherever an erroneous belief, such as the idea of hoopsnakes or of reptiles that swallow their young, gains wide acceptance, there must be some explanation in accord with facts. My belief is that the hoopsnake story had its origin in the ability of blue racers and blacksnakes to run along the ground with their heads lifted for a surprising distance into the air.

When fleeing through tall grass, such snakes sometimes lift their heads higher and higher, the better to see or sense their foes. Possibly glimpses of these reptiles speeding through the waving grass, with heads held so high they seemed bending backward, have given rise to the widespread belief in rolling hoopsnakes.

Similarly that other perennial among serpent misconceptions—the belief that mother snakes swallow their young when danger approaches—may have a simple and logical explanation. When close to the mouth of the burrow, the mother serpent may take her stand, with her head weaving and held close to the ground and her mouth opening in repeated menacing movements, while the little reptiles wriggle down to the comparative safety of their underground retreat. To the excited observer the little snakes—disappearing suddenly from sight—would appear to be rushing into the open mouth of their mother. In fact, instead of their mother, it is the ground which swallows them up.

An interesting instance, illustrating how superstitions start and false premises have their beginning, occurred a mile or so from Lone Oak several years before I appeared on the scene.

On a back-road farm a woman was looking for eggs laid in out-of-the-way places about the barnyard. Coming to a great hollow stump, she leaned over to look inside. A huge "puff adder" was coiled within. With a great hiss, it blew its cloud of "poisonous vapor" directly into her face. The frightened woman ran to the house. On the back of the stove she noticed some neglected toast which had burned to a crisp. She started eating the charred bread, in her distraction, and in a few minutes felt better. The burned toast had proved a miraculous antidote—it had neutralized the venom of the adder!

The story of her escape from death was repeated many times in my boyhood. Burned toast was accepted by numerous people in the region as a sure-cure for the vapor-poison of the puff adder. The weak link in this circumstantial story, as I learned in later years, is the fact that there isn't any puff-adder poison. In fact, there isn't any puff adder!

The great hiss which the woman heard was formed by harmless air; the deadly adder she saw was simply that poor, pitiful pretender, the hog-nosed snake. No more venomous than a kitchen mouse, this reptile tries to frighten its enemies with sound and fury signifying nothing. If they are not intimidated, it flops over on its back and feigns death. This, then, was the sinister, deadly monster which burned toast had miraculously conquered!

How other erroneous beliefs in the realm of natural history, which were current in the dune country at that time, came into being, I do not know. But they were spread, by word of mouth, until acceptance seemed universal. Undoubtedly many were brought to America from the Old Country as representatives of many races lived on the farms of the region. Most of the time, Gramp and Gram quoted folklore beliefs with their tongues in their cheeks. But there were neighbors who clung firmly to the old opinion that bats come down chimneys at night to dine on ham; that snakes suck milk from cows; that a butterfly alighting on a person's head means good luck is coming and that a bird flying into a house indicates important news is on the way.

I remember one Sunday morning when Gram was energetically swatting houseflies with a folded-up piece of newspaper.

"That," said Gramp, looking up from his *Chesterton Tribune*, "makes four hun'red more flies yer bringin' t' th' house. Y've jest killed forty flies an' every time y' kill a fly, ten more come t' its funeral!"

Odd beliefs about insects were many. In numerous ways they were supposed to affect the fortunes of humans. Dream of ants, one superstition stated, and prosperity would come your way. See a ladybug in the house in winter, another declared, and you would receive as many dollars as there were spots on the insect's back. A honeybee buzzing around your head was supposed to indicate a letter was on its way. A measuring worm crawling on a man's shoulder was "measuring him for a shroud." If the same moth larva found its way along a woman's hand, it was "measuring her for new gloves." Thousand-legged worms were thought to crawl into babies' ears and to make them crazy. And dragonflies—usually known as darning needles—were likely, many people affirmed, to sew up the ears of children.

These swift and beautiful insects were associated with numerous other superstitions. They were thought to feed and to doctor snakes and, according to some people, to sting horses. When a country boy went fishing in a place where dragonflies were numerous, he found himself between the horns of a dilemma. If a dragonfly alighted on his pole, it meant the fish wouldn't bite; if he injured a dragonfly, it meant he would have bad luck.

In the lower pasture, near the spring, large numbers of great, tender mushrooms pushed their way above the ground each summer. Gram and I sometimes picked a milkpail full in a quarter of an hour while the morning dew was still on the grass. After removing and discarding the upper skins, Gram would fry them in butter on the kitchen range. When Gramp came in from his chores, we all would enjoy a special treat for breakfast. While we picked the mushrooms in the cool fresh air of the dawn, Gram often told me stories or recalled the queer beliefs she had encountered when she first came west.

A sliver off a hog-trough, many inhabitants of the region

thought, was a sure-cure for a sty. Anyone who saw a boy with his shirttail hanging out would be sure to find a letter waiting for him the next time he went to the post office. If a person's ears grew close to his head, it meant he was stingy; if a person had a large nose, it indicated he possessed a generous nature. In setting the table, if anyone made a mistake and put two knives and no fork at a plate, it presaged a funeral in the family. If, on the other hand, there were two forks and no knife, it indicated the approach of a wedding. Anyone who started off on an errand or a journey and forgot something and had to return, should always sit on a chair before starting out again—otherwise bad luck would follow.

These beliefs, and many more I cannot now recall, were ones that Gram heard in early days. Of all such folklore oddities the ones that interested me most were those which related to the living creatures of the fields and woods.

"Straddle-Bugs," as Gramp called the harvestmen or daddy-longlegs, were thought to have some mystic connection with cattle. Kill a daddy-longlegs, a popular superstition had it, and your cows would go dry. Many a farm-boy, in the dune country, tried the time-honored procedure of holding one of these grandfather-graybeards by two of its legs and noting the direction the others pointed in order to obtain a clew as to the direction taken by strayed cattle.

One summer night, as Gram was reading *When Wilderness Was King* and Gramp and I sat on the front porch outside the screen door, Gramp suddenly exclaimed:

"Listen! There's th' first katydid o' th' year. They say it's just six weeks t' frost from th' time y' hear the first katydid."

Other humble creatures were also imagined to be related in some way to the weather. In autumn the sight of a woolly-bear caterpillar hurrying across an open space indicated that an early winter was on its way. Some country-people maintained, in addition, that you could tell whether the early winter would be mild or severe by examining the central band around its body. A wide band meant a severe winter; a narrow band, a mild one.

"Step on a spider," Gramp used to quote a superstition of the time, "an' it'll rain next day."

"What if you step on a spider on a rainy day?" I once asked.

"Then y'll hev two days o' rain in succession."

Stepping on a cricket was also thought to bring on a rainstorm. I remember that I used to be puzzled by the fact that even the people who quoted this belief never put the prescription to the test by stepping on crickets during a drought.

"All signs fail in dry weather," Gramp explained in answer to my question.

·11·

NEIGHBORS

LIKE the English village of Selborne, immortalized by Gilbert White, Lone Oak and the community around it was singularly isolated although—also like Selborne—it lay hardly more than half a hundred miles from a great center of population. Poor roads discouraged the casual visitor. Teams labored through the sand and travel was slow and burdensome. Only later, with the coming of the automobile in numbers and the improvement of the highways, did the outside world sweep in.

At the time I was a boy the community was composed largely of early settlers, of pioneers, of men and women who had lived and matured as individuals. They were unmolded by advertising, by magazines, by movies, by the radio, or even by extended formal schooling. It was natural, under such conditions, that a number of the inhabitants should be unconventional and unique. Eccentricities were taken for granted and "characters" abounded.

Not far from the little station at Furnessville, old Aunt Mary lived in a rambling frame house set amid maple trees on a hill. She was positive that no house in which she lived would ever burn down.

One late-summer day, when the whole countryside was like tinder from a prolonged drought, Gramp stopped in to see Aunt Mary. He found her calmly burning trash in a low-roofed annex to the kitchen. The pot-bellied stove was cherry red. All around it were high piles of old papers as dry as bleached bones. Nor was that all. A small section of the vertical stovepipe was entirely missing. Shooting flames were streaming from the lower opening, jumping the gap, and—like a thread entering a needle's eye—pouring into the open end of the pipe above.

"Jumpin' Jehosephat!" Gramp shouted. "Yer goin' t' burn yerself t' a cinder!"

Aunt Mary rocked placidly back and forth and added more papers to the blaze.

"Don't y' worry, Uncle Ed," she told him. "Ez long as I'm livin' in this house, it'll never burn down."

Nor did it.

The farmer who occupied the place next to Aunt Mary's was tall and stooped. He had watery blue eyes and a corncob pipe was as much a feature of his countenance as his nose or eyebrows. Except on Sunday, he was clad in ancient clothing at variance with his bank account. Once he caught sight of a tramp leaving the railroad tracks and starting for his house to beg a meal. He sauntered down the path to meet him.

"Goin' t' ask fer somethin' t' eat?" he inquired.

"Yes."

"'Tain't no use. I just come from there. Th' lady wouldn't give me a thing."

As the tramp disappeared down the track, he returned, chuckling, to the house.

At the time of which I write "The Man with the Green Hair" was already becoming one of the legendary characters of the dune country. Known as "Old Sile," he lived with his wife in a dugout at the foot of a sandhill. Where he came from nobody knew. He never spoke of his youth or of his early home. In spite of his poverty, he had polished manners and spoke excellent English with the aid of a wide vocabulary. His wife used to say in a stage whisper:

"Silas is *very* smart. He kin talk on a'most any subject."

In place of a watch, Old Sile used to wear a small alarm clock supported by a steel muskrat-trap chain which encircled his neck. And in the crown of his hat he had a large flat piece of copper. As the years went by the effect of perspiration on the copper dyed his hair a bright green. The metal, Old Sile was convinced, enabled him to pick up electric waves running through the air. By sitting on the top of a sandhill, he said, he could hear everything that was being said in Congress. At Lewrey's Store, at night, he used to tell what was going on in Washington—things that never reached the papers.

In later years Old Sile believed that enemies were seeking to steal his great discovery. He invested part of his scanty savings in a bulletproof vest and used to wear this garment under four shirts, one on top of the other. Obsessed by the idea he might be poisoned, he refused to taste food in any other house than his own—with one exception. That was Lone Oak. He trusted Gram completely and would eat or drink anything she set before him.

The distinguished man of the community was Edwin L. Furness, for whom Furnessville was named. He had moved to Indiana in the early days with a good education and sufficient capital to establish a sawmill and various other enterprises. He was known as "The Gentleman Farmer." He had a private library and his four-story home was the only brick house in the region. The bricks were made from clay dug on his own farm. A magic gate, which opened and closed by itself, was the feature of the driveway which led up the hill to the big red house. I used to examine with the greatest of interest the system of levers and treadles by means of which the wheels of an approaching vehicle swung open the gate and the wheels of a departing one closed it.

In the front yard of the Furness place, a vast expanse of green descending the slope of the hill, I learned one of the important lessons of my life. At Lone Oak, as I have indicated, my labors were desultory and haphazard. I was the Star Boarder. But, I always said to myself, if I ever got a real job and somebody was paying me money for my labors, I would work hard and tend strictly to business. There would be no leaning on the hoe-handle or lying in the shade.

One day, as we were passing the Furness place, the owner, then a slight, elderly man with a snow-white beard trimmed to a point, asked me if I would like to earn some money the next day by mowing the big front lawn. I agreed and by seven o'clock the following morning I was riding my bicycle up the driveway. This was my first paying job. I was no longer working for Gramp and under his beneficent ways. This was the test. I was going to make good.

I started in at top speed and for more than an hour I used sickle and scythe to good effect. When I walked to the spring-house for a drink, I hurried back to my labors. The second trip to the spring-house took longer and the third time I sat down in the cool shade to rest. Long before noon I was working at low speed and guiltily enjoying pauses at increasingly frequent intervals. The afternoon was one long stretch of conscious defeat. I was following the well-worn path of my everyday conduct. My habits were stronger than my determination. I learned that day that the way I handled little things would probably be the way I would handle big things, that my action during commonplace days gave a key to my action during emergencies.

Another of those enduring lessons of childhood had come a little earlier at the Lone Oak grindstone. Helping Gramp sharpen the ax was one of the jobs for which I was corralled from time to time. Very few minutes would pass before my bitter complaints would rise above the shrill whining of the ax.

"Gramp, my back's busted!"

"Can't be. Y've hardly started."

"But it is, honest."

"Nobody ever broke his back turnin' a grindstone."

"I have."

"No y' haven't. Rest yerself by restin' a little more weight on th' handle when y' turn. An' save yer breath."

I would subside and begin counting the turns. One, two, three, four. One, two, three, four . . .

"Gramp, you're riding too hard on the ax!"

"If I don't press down it'll take twi'st as long."

"Why can't I hold the ax and you turn?"

"Y' have t' know how t' hold th' ax."

"I know how. I've been watching you. Let me try."

"Nope. We got t' git done right away. Do y' always have t' quit turnin' when y' talk?"

After a hundred or so more turns I would begin on the oldest of all boy stratagems.

"Gramp!"

"What now?"

"Know what I think?"

"No."

"I think you couldn't keep this grindstone turning as

long as I have."

"Humph! I used t' keep a stone goin' all day long when I was knee-high t' a grasshopper!"

"Yes. Well, let's see you do it now!"

Only once did he fall for this line of tactics.

"All right," he said finally. "Yer so all-fired anxious t' hold th' ax, go ahead an' see what happens."

He spun the wheel until little drops of water shot out like sparks from an emery wheel and I pressed down on the ax.

"Y' can't do all th' sharpenin' on the last quarter-inch," he reminded me. "Y' have t' start further back. An' y' have t' bear down. Y' aren't puttin' on enough weight t' squash a mosquito."

I put on weight. A moment later I shifted the ax awkwardly. A corner, already sharpened, struck the spinning wheel. The resulting gouge ruined the work and I returned ignominiously to the handle. Ruminating as I turned, I realized fully for the first time the importance of knowledge and skill. Throughout life, I saw, it was Skill that rode the ax and Unskill that turned the grindstone.

Across the road from the big, red-brick, hilltop house of the Furnesses lived Ed Morgan. He was a substantial citizen of the community, a descendant of one of its founders. Solid and chunky, he was up—winter and summer—at 5:30 A. M., on the dot.

"My aim in life," he once explained, "has always been th' same—t' git more land."

Acre by acre he added more land to his spreading farm. Taxes rose and the land became a burden. He tried to sell and could find no buyers. During his latter years he lived in a big, frame house in the midst of his many acres with the feeling that things were slipping away from him, were going from bad to worse. However, his head was never bowed nor his spirit of fierce independence broken. Once, when he was well past seventy, I was driving back through the dune country, along the old familiar roads, when I overtook him plodding in the direction of the interurban station. I pulled up and invited him to get in.

"Edwin," he said, "I *can* walk. But I'd be ever so much obliged fer a ride."

Several farms to the east of Lone Oak a green house stood at the top of a small rise. Here lived Dan Sterns. He had been a bachelor until he was long past forty. Finally, to everyone's surprise, he brought home a bride from the other side of Michigan City. As soon as the honeymoon was over, his wife began taking him in hand. When he approached the kitchen door she would shout:

"Wipe off yer feet! An' take off yer hat!"

Soon it became known that she kept a little whip in her lap at mealtime. If Dan reached too far or started to pour his tea in his saucer, she would switch his hands. One noon Gramp stopped on his way home from town to see about some seed corn. Dan was coming disconsolately down the kitchen steps as Gramp drove into the yard. He had just had dinner under the watchful eye of his wife.

"Ed," he burst out, "eatin' ain't eatin' ef a feller can't

eat 'taters with his knife!"

The postmaster at Furnessville was a mild-eyed, inoffensive man related to that swashbuckling Wall-Street plunger, "Bet-You-a-Million" Gates. His name was Henry. He was thin-faced and had a straggly moustache. He always tipped his hat from the back instead of from the front. A bachelor, he lived alone with his mother, who attained the age of ninety and was out of her mind for many of the later years of her life. Several times each night she would get up under the impression that morning had come. Henry would put her back to bed, explaining:

"It isn't morning yet. It's time everybody was in bed."

"Why aren't *you* in bed then?" she would always ask.

Checker-playing was Henry's one avocation. He and a crony would be absorbed in a game in a small room back of the combined post-office and store when a woman would come in to make some purchases. Henry would say:

"Sh! Let's keep quiet an' mebby she'll go away."

He was the nadir of high-pressure salesmanship. He cared little whether people bought anything or not. At sixty-five he was without a wrinkle in his brow. From the windows of his little store he watched the world go by—speeding east and west on the long passenger trains which roared without a stop, through Furnessville.

Half-way to the station, on days when we were rushing to meet the Strawberry Train, we used to pass a frame house with a sandhill rising behind it. A great bite seemed to have been taken out of one side of the dune. The previous owner had considered the sandhill the one blemish on the face of his farm. When he was nearing sixty he set to work with shovel and wheelbarrow. He had determined to haul the whole dune away and dump it in a neighboring swamp.

Month after month, and year after year, he put in his spare time wheeling and grunting, continuing his seemingly endless task. Yet only a small fraction of the great hill of sand had been transported when death relieved him of his self-imposed labors.

His son, Alf, moved into the house and made a living, as best he could, from the farm's arid acres. Years went by and sandburrs and milkweed began to encroach on the open scar on the side of the hill. Then, one day, a stranger stopped at the farmhouse. He explained that he represented a group of Chicago artists who wished to establish a painting colony in the dune country. He was authorized, he said, to pay as high as $10,000 for the place. The picturesque sand-dune had attracted the artists to the farm!

At Lewrey's Store, that night, Alf told of the offer. His neighbors set up a roar of laughter.

"The man's either a swindler or he's crazy," they told him. "You'll never see th' money."

"Well, he looked honest," was all Alf could say.

"Lookin' honest ain't enough!"

But Alf did get the $10,000—in cold cash. He and his wife moved away to Michigan City. For forty years they had been forced to live on a pinchpenny, church-mouse diet. Now they could afford all the food they wanted. Three months later his wife died, the doctor said from the sudden change to rich and plentiful food. At first Alf used to hire a taxicab to bring him back to the old farm just to feed a horde of cats and the seven dogs he had had to leave behind him. Then someone poisoned the dogs, Alf quit coming back, and we saw him no more.

·12·

GALLINIPPERS

A HANDFUL of green grass sifted through my fingers onto the yellow flame of a twig fire. Sudden smoke, gray and acrid, billowed up. In the gathering twilight Gramp and I were sitting beside the driveway, enjoying the cool of the early evening. Bats zigzagged past overhead and the cries of whippoorwills and nighthawks carried from afar. Nearer, just beyond the smoke of our smudge fire, we could hear the high humming of the mosquitoes.

A cranefly drifted past me, its long legs trailing. I ducked. At Lone Oak we assumed that these harmless insects were, in reality, huge mosquitoes and we called them gallinippers. The sight of the cranefly reminded Gramp of Mr. Bump and of his encounter with the world's biggest mosquito.

"One time," he said, "Mr. Bump stopped at a tavern an' fell in with two strangers. Both o' 'em were little fellers, no bigger'n a bar o' soap after a hard day's wash. But they was big talkers. All three o' 'em began swappin' lies. The first stranger said:

" 'Where I come from the soil is so rich everythin' grows extra-big. I once raised a cabbage so big that when a rainstorm came up I drove my team an' my lumber wagon under one side o' thet cabbage an' not a drop o' rain touched us!'

" 'Thet certainly was a big cabbage!' says th' second stranger. 'I never saw anything like it. But I'll tell y' what I did see. One time I passed an iron works where a thousan' men were workin' on one iron kettle. An' thet kettle was so large thet each man was so far away from his nearest neighbor thet he couldn't make him hear by yellin' his loudest!'

" 'Well,' said the first man, 'thet *was* a big kettle. What was they goin' t' do with it?'

" 'Cook your cabbage!'

"Then Mr. Bump spoke up. He said:

" 'Gentlemen, this is strange indeed. I was one of the workmen on thet very kettle! An' a curious thing happened t' me when 't was almost finished. As I was leavin' work one evenin' th' biggest gallinipper in all th' world took out after me. I ran under th' iron kettle an' thet skeeter bored right through th' side. I grabbed a sledge-hammer an' pounded away 'til I clinched its beak over inside th' kettle. Then I ran t' git a cannon t' kill th' galli-nipper. But 'pon my honor, gentlemen, I hadn't gone a hundred yards before thet mosquito flew off with th' kettle!' "

When my laughter and Gramp's chuckles had died away, we remained silent listening to the first fiddling of the night insects. Crickets chirped from the grass-tangles. Katydids, among the bushes, began their endless affirmations and denials. The mellow notes of the snowy tree crickets carried from the grape arbor. And, away across the meadows and marshland, the shrill orchestration of the nocturnal grasshoppers grew in volume.

As each night advanced, the shrilling of these insects rose to a crescendo. To anyone unfamiliar with its source, the vast, ear-piercing tumult would have been a cause for quakings and alarm. Years before, a distant relative from Chicago, a young woman who had never spent a night out of the city before, came to stay a week at Lone Oak. The next morning she took the train back to Chicago. She had spent a night of terror, assailed by a shrill confusion of wild and direful sounds outside her window.

My introduction to the insects, like that of most people, began with the less-desirable species—the biting flies and the lance-beaked mosquitoes. They sought me out. It was only later that I grew to know their many shy and beautiful, harmless and endlessly interesting relatives. I have told in another volume, *Grassroot Jungles,* of my first memorable vision of insect beauty, when I came upon two ethereal creatures, pale green and with flowing ribbon-tails, clinging to the leaves of the grape arbor. These luna moths seemed like delicate dancers from some Cinderella's ball.

In a lower hay-field one summer, when I was helping turn over red clover, I encountered another gorgeous moth of the night, a Polyphemus with a wingspread of nearly half a foot. The hawk moths, which hung on vibrating wings while their sucking tongues—longer than their bodies—uncurled and plumbed the depths of the trumpet-shaped flowers in Gram's front yard, aroused my early interest also. These humming birds of the night often hovered within reach of my hand as I stood unmoving beside the hollyhocks or among the phlox.

There was one year, I believe 1911, when curious insect occurrences of several kinds attracted my attention. Maple trees all over Lone Oak suddenly seemed to sprout pussy willows along their twigs. A scale insect which created masses of white, cottony material had attacked the trees. Later that summer there was a curious "butterfly storm." All one day the air seemed filled with fluttering forms—not of one species but of many kinds: yellow, brown, white, speckled, striped, mottled and plain. Then there was the case of the unintelligent fly.

One morning, about nine o'clock, I saw this housefly descend into the top of an unused lamp chimney. It explored downward until it came to the sharp bulge of the lower portion. Then it began flying around and around.

At noon I saw it was still bumping along the inside of the glass, unable to find its way to freedom. That night it remained a prisoner. The next morning I found it buzzing aimlessly about where I had seen it the day before. It still lacked sufficient sense to make its escape through the open top of the chimney above it. Taking pity on it, I carried its transparent prison-house outdoors and shook the fly free.

After the asparagus season was over, each year, Gramp permitted the plants to grow up into a feathery green tangle. I used to lie on my back, looking up at the fern-like branches, with their round, red berries, as though exploring in the midst of some strange tropical jungle. Odd little beetles, with shining, metallic coats-of-mail, ran among the treetops of the asparagus-forest. Small flies on blurring wings moved among the greenery and, from time to time, a sudden shock would shake the plant as a grasshopper landed with an impact upon the slender stalk.

What the multiform insects around me were I could only guess. To the farmers of the region all flies were simply "flies," all grasshoppers were "hoppers," and all insects were "bugs." In *Steele's Popular Zoology* there was a short section devoted to entomology and in the Lone Oak dictionary some of the most striking butterflies were pictured. One other aid to identification should be mentioned.

Each year the mailman deposited in Gramp's mailbox tangible evidence that the Government in Washington had not forgotten him. The annual yearbook of the U.S. Department of Agriculture arrived. For many years it was bound in blue and had letters of gold stamped on the cover. Most of the articles inside proved dreary reading for one of my temperament, but occasionally there would be a natural-history oasis, a page of colored plates, an article on the agricultural value of birds, or the life-story of some insect. Outstanding in my memory are the colored plates of new fruits and of insects. To be sure, most of the insects were pests, agricultural enemies, fiends with six legs. They were shown in the colored pictures consuming peaches, boring into roots, nibbling on leaves, destroying ears of corn, sapping the lifeblood of agricultural plants.

Even so, there were fascinating facts about some of the small creatures and about their incredibly cunning ruses for evading the penalty of their crimes. The life cycles of the harmful insects, as given in these annual volumes, provided me with my first entomological literature. It was, admittedly, an unbalanced diet, a one-sided presentation of the case. There was only rare mention, in passing, of the immense benefits conferred by many species of insects upon farms and farmers. Occasional bulletins from the state department of agriculture, in Indianapolis, abetted this viewpoint. However, nothing in these latter publications ever proved of as much interest as the seal of the State of Indiana printed on the back cover. I used to look at it for long periods. It showed a woodsman chopping at a huge tree while a bison charged past and a great sun rose behind them. Somehow that small circular picture epitomized to me the glory and romance of the early days.

Usually, by the time the twig-fire in the driveway burned itself out, and the lessening of the smoke permitted the mosquitoes to rush in to the attack, Gram would be ready to read and we would retire within the protection of the screened windows and doors. Sometimes, attracted by the lamplight, moths from the neighboring woods and marshes would flutter their silken wings along the mesh of the screens. And after the reading was over, and I had climbed the stairs to my bedroom, the last sound I heard each night was the chorus of the insects.

I remember one evening in particular. My small bedroom window looked out into the east, into a world of silver mist flooded with moonlight from a great round moon rising above the big maple. From marsh and meadow swelled the vast song of the night insects. The shrillness was gone. It seemed softened and subdued by the mist. And from afar came the sound of a concertina breathing exotic, old-world music at the farm of distant Polanders. And then there was the soft yielding of the feather-bed around me and the great moon at my window pouring golden thistledown over me and the faraway bark of a dog and the thin reiteration of "Katydid! Katydidn't!" and I was fast asleep.

·13·

DINNER BELLS

"I DON'T git hungry very often. But when I do 'ts about *now.*"

Gramp pulled out his gold watch.

"How-some-ever," he added, " 'ts only eleven-thirty. I 'spect we'd better finish th' row."

We were hoeing corn in July. The smell of the hot sand rose to our nostrils as we sliced and chopped among the small weeds.

"If we pull up some weeds, cut some off, an' stomp some down, I reckon th' rest will die," Gramp said.

We hoed on in silence for several minutes. Gramp

looked at his watch again.

"I rec'lect one time when Mr. Bump was in th' army. 'Twas a hot day like this. Th' Gin'ral lined up all th' soldiers an' said: 'Now men, our ammunition is gittin' low. I want y' t' fire an' keep on firin' 'til yer last ca'tridge is gone. Then run.' Mr. Bump saluted. 'Gin'ral,' he said, 'I'm a little lame. I think I'll start now!'

"I feel a mite lame, myself," Gramp concluded. "Mebby we better start fer th' house now or we might be late fer dinner."

On several of the neighboring farms large dinner bells were mounted on posts near the kitchen door for summoning workers from the fields at mealtime. There was no such bell at Lone Oak. Gramp didn't need any. He was always there—usually a little ahead of time.

Our arrival at the kitchen door was our second appearance there that morning. About ten o'clock Gramp always came to the house "for a drink of water." I always stopped whatever work or play I was engaged in and joined him. For the drink of water invariably led to a glass of ice-cold buttermilk from the cellar and that called for a handful of soda-crackers and the complement of the crackers was a slice of what Gramp called "rat cheese." When this snack was over, Gramp would return to his labors and I would resume my activities where I had left them.

During those summers I was insatiably fond of fruits of all kinds. Looking back, it seems that, in fruit season, I ate from morning until night. I would wander from dewberry vines to blackberry bushes and from plum trees to peach trees. During "in between" spells, when fruit was ripening, I would beg Gram for raisins. She doled them out to me twelve at a time. During my earliest years the only name I knew for raisins was "twelve."

The Lone Oak pantry, from which the "twelve" came, had many other enticements beside raisins. There were rows of small jelly jars, a large tin box holding the loaves of snow-white bread which Gram baked each Wednesday and Saturday, glass containers filled with fried-cakes and oatmeal cookies, and often besides there were berry pies, gingerbread, cinnamon rolls, or newly baked Johnny-cake.

The contents of the pantry, however, was a mere sample of the vast store of provender packed in the cellar during winter months.

Each autumn Gram seemed preparing for a siege. She stored the underground room with an almost incredible amount of eatables. Bins and boxes and barrels were packed to capacity. Battalions of glass jars held canned pears and plums and peaches and cherries, strawberries and huckleberries and raspberries. The mainstays of the canned vegetable section were peas, tomatoes, string beans, and sweet corn. Jelly jars held four flavors: apple, grape, crabapple, and cranberry. Other containers were filled with watermelon, peach, cherry, and strawberry preserves.

I remember a specialty of Gram's was carrot marmalade. How she produced this delicacy remained a mystery to me until very recently. Then I found the receipt written in her own hand on a blank page in the ancient, brown-covered cookbook she used when I was a boy. I copy it as she wrote it:

Carrot Marmalade

2 lbs. of carrots cleaned and run through a food-cutter.
3 lemons cut with the finest cutter.
Cover each with water and cook separately for ½ hour.
Then put together and add 6 cups of sugar and 1½ cups of corn syrup.
Cook until clear.

Another of these old receipts brought back a flood of pleasant memories. It gave directions for making "No Name Cake." Gram's instructions run as follows:

No Name Cake

1 cup butter	4 cups flour
2 cups sugar	3 teaspoons baking powder
3 eggs	Or, 1 teaspoon of soda and 2 of cream tartar
1 cup milk	

Mix ingredients in the order given. Divide into three parts and to one-third of the mixture add the following:

1 cup raisins and currants mixed and chopped
2 tablespoons molasses
¼ teaspoon grated nutmeg
1 teaspoon each, cinnamon, cloves, and vanilla

Bake in shallow tins, putting the dark layer between the light ones with icing.

Up until Thanksgiving time plump bunches of fresh

Concord grapes could be brought up from the marvelous Lone Oak cellar. They were packed in a box of sawdust with the ends of the stems sealed with wax. Another box held perfect Northern Spy and Baldwin apples, polished and wrapped in pieces of newspaper. They were being saved for decorating the Christmas tree. The eating apples were ranged in barrels along one cellar-wall. Gunny sacks bulged with dry onions, baskets were heaping full of carrots, a large bin held the late potatoes. Surplus potatoes, cabbage, and russet apples were stored in an outdoor root cellar.

Every fall Gramp butchered two of the choicest pigs. The boiling pork was put down in salt brine in a barrel, the bacon was smoked in a small, almost air-tight smokehouse, and the hams were dry-cured, English style, by treating them with salt, flour, sugar, and saltpeter. The selected hams were first rubbed well with salt, then set away for three days. At the end of that time Gram rubbed them again with salt to which sugar had been added in the proportions of two to one. Beside each knuckle-joint she made a deep hole into which she inserted a bean-sized piece of saltpeter. Then she filled the hole with salt. Placed on a long table, the hams were turned every other day for ten days. Then flour, to which a little pepper had been added, was rubbed thoroughly into the outside of each ham. The final step was covering the hams with cheesecloth and hanging them from the ceiling of the cellar.

A large stone jar of pork sausage, well seasoned with

home-grown sage, was the product of odds and ends during the butchering. When all the meat was packed away, it was not unusual to have as many as fifty or sixty pounds of lard. There was little danger of having too much, for there was a constant call for it in making pies and doughnuts.

In one corner of the cellar two large kegs held cucumber pickles. The first keg contained small cucumbers, two or two and a half inches long. They were packed in spiced and sweetened vinegar to which a little alum was added. It kept the sweet pickles crisp. The second keg held salt brine and larger cucumbers, from four to five inches in length. They were packed layer on layer in the brine. Gram used to test the strength of the brine by putting a fresh egg in it. If the egg floated, the salt solution was sufficiently strong.

Every second day, during the cucumber season, pickles fresh from the vines were added to the barrel. A flat stone held all the cucumbers below the surface. When the barrel was full, a thick layer of fresh grape-leaves was placed on top and the keg was covered with a cloth. During winter months these large pickles were brought up, a small panful at a time, and soaked in clear water over night. Then they were cut in halves and covered with vinegar to which had been added a pinch of brown sugar.

These two kinds of pickles, however, were only the beginning. Gram's cellar was the repository of a wide variety of relishes. There were pickled peaches, a clove stuck in the side of each. There were spiced crabapples, each with its own slender stem. There were almost transparent watermelon pickles, green tomato pickles—with a slight flavor of onion—sweet apple pickles—cut into quarters and rich in their own spiced juices. There were small pickled pears, for serving with ham, and long, tender string-bean pickles, for serving with boiled beef. And, row on row, bottles and jars held catsup, chili sauce, and piccalilli.

Each autumn Gramp had a barrel of cider made at the Furnessville cider-mill. Gram boiled several gallons and sealed it in two-quart jars for use as a winter beverage. The rest was put in a corner of the cellar to ferment and form vinegar, most of which Gramp sold when spring came. Invariably Gram placed several rolls of heavy brown paper in the barrel of fermenting cider. This, she said, formed "mother" and aided in its transformation into vinegar.

On winter nights a trip down cellar after apples or cider was an olfactory adventure of the highest odor. The smell of the kerosene lamp mingled with the delicious odor of stored fruit, the earthy smell of the potato bin, the heavy scent of the pickle-kegs, the hundred and one other perfumes of this storehouse of food.

None of this food was wasted and all of it was enjoyed. At Lone Oak mealtime was no ordinary affair. Gramp saw to that. Warm food nourished his memory and his wit as well as his body. As we ate, he often recalled stories and events of his own youthful days.

For several years after his family moved west to Indiana they lived in the home of penurious relatives. At the table his aunt always sat with the sugar bowl in her lap, doling out small helpings with extreme reluctance. Although his father was paying all the food bills, every mouthful was carefully watched. Gramp was growing like a weed and was always hungry.

Once his aunt had watched the food disappear and had exclaimed in exasperation: "I wish ten thousand like our Ed was drove t' Jerusalem!"

Another time his uncle complained bitterly: "Ed Way, you'd *breed* a famine!"

"Up until the time I was sixteen," Gramp once told me, "I didn't know chickens had anything but necks and wings."

When he was fourteen he was sent to a neighbor's house on an errand around noontime. The neighbor invited: "Bub, pull up a chair an' sit in."

Gramp thought he ought to be polite, so he said: "No thank y'. I'm not hungry."

The neighbor took him at his word and he nearly starved to death watching them eat.

"I've *never* refused an invitation t' eat since!" Gramp concluded that story.

On another occasion, when he had hired out as a sixteen-year-old to chop wood, he was invited to dinner at his employer's house. Gramp was not conscious of eating more than anyone else. But at the end of five minutes the man spoke up:

"That's right," he said. "I like t' see a man *eat* when he sits down t' my table!"

DINNER BELLS

In a good many of the dune-country farmhouses far more thought was given to the money-value of the food consumed than was the case at Lone Oak. Gramp once expressed his attitude as follows:

"When I can't hev what I want t' *eat* without thinkin' o' th' *cost,* it'll be time t' die!"

Gram's reputation as a cook was widespread and friends visited Lone Oak from as far away as Valparaiso. They were always welcome. When company was coming, there would be several days of dusting and sweeping and washing. Gramp and I had to watch our step. To Gramp's way of thinking, this was largely a waste of energy. No preparations at all should be necessary—for friends. He was like Socrates, who replied when upbraided by his wife, Xanthippe, for his lack of preparations for receiving guests:

"If they are our friends, they will not care about it; if they are not, we shall not care about them."

Immensely proud of Gram's ability in the kitchen, Gramp was given to teasing her when company came.

"We don't make any excuses fer th' food here," he would explain, beaming jovially on the assembled company. "What's good enough fer us *all th' time* ought t' be good enough fer y' fer just *one meal!*"

That, I knew, was only a starter and I wiggled my toes in pleasurable anticipation of what was coming.

"The Good Book," Gramp remarked a little later in the meal, "the Good Book says ye shall not live by bread alone. But I'll take a slice, Edwin, ef y' don't mind."

The bread reminded him of the first loaf Gram had baked after they were married.

"She was just gettin' her hand in then," he explained. "I ate a slice an' I didn't know just what t' say. So I was truthful an' complimentary, too. I said: 'This isn't th' *worst* bread I ever ate—but it isn't the *best,* either!'

"But," he put in hastily, "there's always somethin' about Mother's bread that tastes like more."

What he was likely to say next none of us knew. Once when someone asked him: "How's the jam, Mr. Way?" he replied: "Well, as th' feller said, 'ts good enough what there is of it, an' enough of it unless it's better!"

His soft voice, his ready smile, his joking manner, his obvious good nature disarmed everyone. They eliminated the possibility of offense. Nobody ever thought of taking exception to one of "Uncle Ed's speeches."

About this time olives had made their first appearance on the table at Lone Oak. Gramp viewed them with mild disfavor. He consumed his full share but with many a dubious shake of the head. Finally he observed:

"Some things are like a singed cat: They taste better'n they look. These olives *look* all right. But they certainly *taste* like next t' nawthin'."

Toward the end of the meal—after the heaped-up mountains of beaten potatoes, holding golden and melting chunks of butter, had descended to mere foothills and after the great platter of fried chicken had reached the lower stratum devoted to necks and wings and "the part of the chicken that jumped over the fence last"—two kinds of juicy berry pie would begin making the rounds. This was the moment I had been awaiting with a mounting sense of despair as I realized that my capacity was lessening rapidly.

Gramp appeared to be filled with no such emotions. He would carefully help himself to an oversized wedge of pie, eat it with evident relish, and then inquire blandly:

"Could I have a piece o' pie? The sample was pretty good!"

Later in the day, after the meal was over and the afternoon had worn on and the guests were climbing into their buggies to depart, Gramp would urge them, in characteristic fashion, to come again.

"Th' next time, come over some Saturday night, bring yer supper an' stay all week!"

The friends would drive away in laughter. As they turned to wave good-by, he would speed the departing guests with a final sally:

"An' don't forget—ef y' ever git within a *mile* o' our house again, be sure an' STOP!"

·14·

GREAT WINDS

IN THE dusk of summer nights, when the great barn was filling with blackness and streams of milk drove downward with a soft, purring sound into Gramp's tin pail, I used to wander out into the coolness of the barnyard. There I would perch on the top pole of the bars and watch the Lone Oak swallows.

This was an evening rite to which I looked forward. The grace of the birds, the swift shuttling of their flight, their bright twittering cries, and their sudden fluttering stops in mid-air—all these were a continual source of enjoyment. No other bird I knew had such grace or exhibited so clearly the delights of flying. I used to twist and turn, almost losing my balance on the bars, as I followed the wheel and skim of their sure evolutions. The birds became accustomed to my presence; they would sweep past almost within reach of my hand.

Watching them, as I did night after night, I began to long with increasing intensity for wings of my own. Sitting on the poplar bar, with its bark half worn away by the rubbing of the cattle, I used to imagine how I would speed above the barn and the hemlock tree, how I would circle the farmhouse, how I would shoot down an aerial toboggan over the old spring, how I would climb up and up and then descend in a dizzying spiral as though sliding down the banister of a stairway in the sky.

On other days, when cumulus clouds reared into the sultry sky all around the horizon and hung there, like white-clad giants resting their elbows on the rim of the world, I would lie in the meadow-grass and spend hours on end dreaming of the joys of riding on wings through their magical realm.

And so it came about, when I was ten years old, that I determined to fly.

Navigation of the air was then just beginning. The world's first air-meet, at Rheims, France, had been held but the year before. The great pioneers of human flight, the Wright brothers, A. Santos-Dumont, Louis Blériot, Henri Farman, Glenn Curtiss, all were still making aerial history and newspaper headlines. The headless Wright biplane was then a new departure.

With all the intensity of enthusiasm with which I turned to each new interest, I plunged into aeronautics. Every book in the Michigan City Library which even skirted the subject I read again and again. During a single summer I read *My Airships,* by Alberto Santos-Dumont, nine times. *Vehicles of the Air,* by Victor Lougheed, *My Three Big Flights,* by André Beaumont, and *The Conquest of the Air,* by Alphonse Berget, were the starting points of a thousand day-dreams. An uncle of mine, who lived in California, sent me a stray copy of *Aircraft Magazine* and I literally wore it to pieces reading each word over and over again and studying each picture innumerable times.

In this reading I solved a mystery of several years' standing. One Christmas vacation, when I was six or so, some neighbors arrived for a Sunday-evening call—stamping off the snow at the door and rubbing their hands together over the comforting dull red spot on the top of the kitchen range. After a bowl of Christmas doughnuts and a plate of Northern Spy apples—carefully polished on Gram's apron—had begun making the rounds, one of the men recalled the story of "The Crazy Old Man of the Sand-Dunes."

It seemed that some years before he had appeared in the dune-country and had established a camp near a lofty sandhill which sloped away toward the lake. From the top of this dune it was his wont to leap into the air with artificial wings and to go sailing down the slope in an effort to fly. His first wings, it was said, had been thatched with chicken feathers. Later ones were pure white and made of pine and muslin.

No story I had ever heard impressed me more deeply. For many nights afterward as I snuggled down in the woolen blankets of a cold bedroom, rubbing my feet rapidly back and forth to warm them by friction, I thought of this lonely old man and of his efforts to fly. I could picture him vividly in my mind's eye—soaring above that long slope of yellow sand, out above the tawny beach and the blue and white of the breakers. I could see his long white beard trailing behind in the wind and I could hear the gulls screaming in the sky around him as he rode through the air on wings of his own making.

And now, in my aviation books, I learned who this "crazy man" really was. He was Octave Chanute, one of the outstanding pioneers of human flight. As chief engineer of the Santa Fe Railroad he built the first bridge across the lower Missouri. The city of Chanute, Kansas, was named in his honor. In later years, when I once interviewed Orville Wright, I learned that Chanute's work, so unappreciated by the dune-country dwellers, had formed a cornerstone of later research. Just before the Wright brothers first flew in 1903, Octave Chanute was a guest at their Kitty Hawk camp among those other sand-dunes on the Carolina coast.

The hill from which Chanute had launched himself on his earliest fledgling wings lay but a few miles from Lone Oak Farm. Discovery of this fact increased still further my desire to be an aerial pioneer myself.

With whittled white pine, pliable gray baling wire, and

white paper held in place with flour-and-water paste, I began reproducing the early planes of the world in little machines with a foot or so wing-span. Gramp's woodshed became the hangar in which I stored these miniature reproductions of the winged craft which filled my dreams —models of Wright and Curtiss and Farman biplanes, of Antoinette and Blériot and Demoiselle monoplanes, of racing Hanriots and wing-clipped Nieuports. In neck-and-neck races I banked my little ships around the pylons formed by Gram's clothespoles. Cross-country flights carried me out over the fluffy green forest of the late-summer asparagus patch, above the Grand Canyons of the ditches, and across the mountains of the potato hills.

Small helicopters, which I made by cutting lifting blades from the sides of empty tin cans, sometimes rose straight upward for half the height of the great oak tree. Once a gust caught one of these soaring pieces of tin and carried it, shining in the sun, over the ridge of the farmhouse as though it were a plane crossing the backbone of the Rockies. On another day, when I was flying a toy helicopter near an apple tree, a kingbird, nesting there, took exception to the whirling piece of metal. With a shrill cry, it darted fearlessly toward it. Hardly six inches from the spinning dangerous blades it tilted and veered away, rising again to its apple-bough perch. Each time I sent the piece of tin aloft the bird swooped downward, screaming, and tried to frighten it away.

About this time I began wearing my cap backwards in the manner of my great aerial heroes, Hubert Latham and

Lincoln Beachey. I also put myself through manifold tests to prove my fitness for a career in the air. Once, I remember, I hung for seventy-five seconds head-downward from an apple-limb to discover the sensations of flying upside-down. On another occasion I stuck my head out of the window of an inter-urban train going sixty miles an hour to find out if I could see without goggles at high speeds. The most memorable feature of that experiment came the following morning. When I awoke I couldn't open my eyes. I had caught cold in them. My eyelids were puffed up like doorknobs.

On those occasions when Gramp let me take the clattering mowing machine for a round or two of the hayfield I used to imagine that the noise was the roar of an air-cooled motor and my bumping progress was produced by air-pockets in the sky. Sometimes I climbed to the very peak of the great red barn and, holding my breath, peered downward from a dizzy height of more than thirty feet. But always it was the poetry of flight rather than the mathematics of flight which interested me. It was dreams of entering a new world of nature—the sky-world of the birds—which attracted me most.

During later years, on magazine assignments, I flew thousands of miles in many kinds of aircraft—in training planes and flying boats, in experimental ships and autogiros, in bombers and sky-liners. Only twice did I experience the sensation of flight as I had imagined it. Once was when our plane slipped silently downward through fleecy clouds with the engine idling. The other time came during that moment of calm, with the wind lisping along the wings, when the plane—losing its flying speed—drifts through the sky for the fraction of a minute before it falls away into the gyrating terror of the tailspin.

Occasionally, during midsummer days at Lone Oak, a time of sudden excitement and change was heralded by thunderheads mushrooming upward beyond the sand-dunes. Cattle grew restless in the fields. Flies and gnats bit with redoubled hunger. Birds darted from tree to tree. And I, like one of these natural creatures, felt in my bones the coming of the storm.

It was on such days that I came nearest of all to experiencing the sensation of flight as I imagined it—the wild rush of the wind, the exhilarating lift from the rut of commonplace days. It was my habit when a storm approached over the lake from the northwest, and the prevailing wind struck with sudden gusts and fury, to take my place on the brow of the hill where the cherry orchard dropped away to a wide expanse of marshland. Here I was exposed to the full fury of the blasts. Elevated above the green lowland which stretched away to the tracks of the Père Marquette Railroad, and with the gale roaring and buffeting around me, I could taste to the full the sensation of rushing through the air and, in imagination, soaring out over the marsh below.

I recall a passage in one of the books of W. H. Hudson, *Nature in Downland,* in which the author tells of the pleasure he felt in a somewhat similar sensation, experienced among the rolling hills of Sussex.

"That desire," he says, "which we all have at times for wings . . . most often comes to me on these great green hills. Looking across vast intervening hollows to other rounded heights and hills beyond and far away, the wish is more than a wish, and I can almost realize the sensation of being other than I am—a creature with the instinct of flight and the correlated faculty; that in a little while, when I have gazed my full and am ready to change my place, I shall lift great heron-like wings and fly with little effort to other points of view."

On my orchard hillside, beneath a darkening sky, I used to race about, breathing in the fresh lake-smell which came with the wind, climbing among the tossing branches of the cherry trees. Great winds from the northwest, booming through the trees, found a response in my nervous system. In this emotion I imagined myself for many years peculiar and alone. Then I came upon John Muir's account of a great night storm in a western forest in which he relates his intense delight in climbing among the trees as they bent like bows under the buffetings of the wind. Here was a kindred spirit, one who knew as I knew the joy of battling amid the pounding surf of the air.

Even after the rain—cold and hard and driven by the gusts—began pelting on my cotton shirt, I used to run across the hillside until, breathless, I would return to the farmhouse in the downpour. Some deep need of the spirit, some inheritance of untold centuries, was finding release in this contact with the sky-wind.

Gram used to maintain that I would "catch my death

of cold" and Gramp made frequent references to people "who didn't know enough to come in out of the rain." He also told, in lurid detail, stories about boys who climbed trees and had been struck by lightning during thunderstorms. But both seemed to realize instinctively that in some understandable manner a very puzzling small boy was finding the answer to an ill-defined and individual need in this strange behavior.

It was thus, through the swift shuttling of the barnyard swallows, through the high-piled sky-mountains of the cumulus clouds, through the rush and buffet of the great winds, that my longing to fly was constantly fed. It was during my thirteenth summer that this longing reached its climax in the twenty-four-foot wings and the covered-in fuselage of *The Dragonette.*

·15·

SKY RACE

IT WAS while I was in the midst of this great project that exciting news appeared in the papers. *Aero and Hydro,* an aviation magazine published in Chicago, had announced a race around the Great Lakes from Chicago to Detroit. Hydroaeroplanes and flying boats from all over the country would compete. Glenn L. Martin was bringing a new-model tractor biplane from California; Tony Jannus was coming from St. Louis with a Benoist flying boat; Roy M. Francis had entered a huge biplane pulled by twin tractor propellers; and Beckwith Havens, a handsome young Easterner, was to be at the controls of the latest-model Curtiss flying boat. The race was to start on the eighth of July and the first stop was to be Michigan City.

As the day approached my excitement mounted. The biggest days on my calendar were Christmas and the Fourth of July. But this year the Fourth was eclipsed completely. The Eighth of July became the superlative day of the summer. I saved up my money for the great event.

I oiled my bicycle the night before and began pedaling the six miles of sand and gravel road to the city shortly after daybreak. I was taking no chances on a repetition of events at a previous race. Two years before, the feature of a Fourth of July celebration had been a motorcycle race from Michigan City to Laporte. I had pedaled the twelve miles, round trip, to see the great event.

Starting a little late, I reached the main street after a large crowd had collected. The machines were already at the starting line, their motors idling. But they were completely hidden by the crowd. I saw the starter's hand, holding a shining pistol, rise above the heads in front of me. A tiny puff of blue smoke spurted from the muzzle. The racing machines volleyed like machine-guns. A great cloud of dust and engine-fumes swirled around us. The roar of the engines diminished with distance. Still I could see nothing. Finally, standing on tip-toe, I caught a fleeting glimpse of the motorcycles, bunched together and moving in a cloud of dust as though in a whirlwind, disappearing down a side-street. That was all I saw of the race.

As I left the farmhouse, Gramp was on his way to the morning milking.

"Y' remind me o' the time I went t' Laporte fer th' Fourth of July," he remarked. "I was a young'n then, too, and so all-fired afraid I'd miss some o' th' doings that I got up at cock-crow. Then, when I got t' Laporte, I was so scairt I'd miss th' train home in th' evening thet I sat in th' station 'most all day long!"

When my bicycle rolled down the main street of Michigan City, milkmen were still abroad. The sidewalks were deserted. The decorations, put up the day before, hung limp and wet with dew. I headed for the lake-front park where the racing planes would come in. A large area had been roped off. I sat on a bench and figured up the number of minutes until noon, when the machines were expected to arrive. Then I roamed about town, watching the city awaken.

As soon as the Canditorium opened its doors I was on hand to order an ice cream soda. Making it last as long as possible, I was surprised to find it was still only eight-thirty when I finished. But now activity was picking up. At the park, pop and ice cream cones and popcorn and peanuts were being displayed at stands. Sandwiches and milk went on sale. Men with canes and flags and souvenirs hawked their wares. And from a wrinkled, red-cheeked little man, who was pushing a red-white-and-blue barrel mounted on two wheels, came the reiterated cry:

"Lemonade! Lemonade!
Made in the shade!

Stirred by an old maid!
Lemonade! Lemonade"

By eating and drinking, like the sons of Job, I whiled away the morning. I had a glass of lemonade, then I tried a sandwich and a glass of milk, then a bag of popcorn, then a bottle of cherry pop, followed by some sticks of "patriotic red, white, and blue candy." I walked back to the Canditorium and this time had a sarsaparilla soda. Then, remembering that the planes might come in at noon, I decided the wise thing might be to eat my dinner at eleven o'clock. Then I wouldn't get hungry in the middle of the excitement.

By the end of the meal, which I finished off with an immense slice of watermelon crisp from the icebox, the hands of the clock stood at 11:40. I hurried down the street and across the bridge to the park. Already a scattering crowd was lined up along the rope barrier. I wormed into the front line and settled down to enjoy the supreme thrill of seeing my first air-and-water craft in flight.

An hour passed. Word came in that Martin was balked at the starting-line by magneto trouble. Francis was temporarily out of the race with a damaged propeller. But Jannus and Havens had lifted from the water of the Chicago lakefront and were on their way. Every distant gull produced a false alarm. Officials read a second announcement. Jannus was down near Gary with a broken propeller; Havens hadn't been seen since starting. My heart sank. Maybe none of the machines would get through to

Michigan City. The man next to me puffed away endlessly, filling the air with the sweet sickish odor of Turkish cigarettes. It was a new odor to me and one I didn't like. The ice cream sodas, sandwiches, watermelon, popcorn, lemonade, candy, and cherry pop lay in uneasy confinement. I felt very depressed.

Then a great shout lifted around me and I forgot everything in a surge of excitement.

"There he is! There he is!" shouted the crowd.

I swept my eyes across the sky but could see nothing. Then I caught sight of the flying boat coming in low over the water, skimming like a great gull just above the waves. It headed directly toward us, crossed the finish line, wheeled upward in a wide circle, slid down, skimmed the water with the wave-tops spanking along its hull, plowed into the lake in a sudden burst of white spray and then idled straight inshore. At 1:40 P. M. the machine slid up on the wet sand. The high-pitched thunder of the motor stopped and the sudden silence was broken by shouts and handclapping. The winged boat had made the trip from Chicago at a speed of approximately a mile a minute.

Two men climbed out stiffly. One was Havens. The other was J. B. R. Verplanck, his passenger and the owner of the plane. I was all eyes. Havens had his shirt-sleeves rolled up and around his left wrist was a band of black leather holding the first wrist-watch I had ever seen. While he talked to officials and had the flying boat pulled to higher ground, a band concert began behind us and most of the crowd wandered away. I slipped quietly under the rope and viewed the craft in awed silence.

The breeze had freshened. An ominous haze spread over the northwestern sky and the distant muttering of thunder carried across the lake. Dust-devils swirled along the sand. Havens and Verplanck looked anxiously at the sky from time to time. Suddenly the storm came. The glare of the sun disappeared in scudding clouds and hard drops of rain pockmarked the dry sand and pounded on the taut wings of the flying boat. The wind came in great gusts from the open water. Under the sudden violence of the gale the flying boat rocked wildly. The men nearest grabbed struts and guy-wires, holding the machine steady while other men got ropes and stakes. I was reaching for one of the wing-tip struts when Havens came past.

"That's the boy!" he encouraged. "Can you hang on there until we stake her down?"

"Sure I can," I told him. I felt a glow run like a wave along my body. I had talked to an aviator!

Clinging to that varnished and streamlined strut was like touching one of the feathers of Pegasus. It was part of a winged craft which, but a few minutes before, had been sailing through the sky. I stuck to my place until the sudden tempest was over, until the worrying of the wind had ceased. In the sudden sunlight, which shot downward from a rift in the clouds, the machine looked more beautiful than ever, its wet wings and hull shining like new leaves in the sun.

Bursting with news, I mounted my drenched bicycle

and started for home. Hardly had I left the city limits before the temperamental weather turned stormy again. In one of the most violent thunderstorms of the summer, the wind boomed and shrieked around me. At times it held me motionless, although I pedaled with all my might into the teeth of the gale. Once I rounded a corner and met the wind broadside as it swept across an open field. Banked over at a steep angle, as though rounding a fast curve, I traveled for a quarter of a mile down a straight stretch of road, supported by the great wind. This sport was as thrilling as flying!

Although the lightning ran in jagged streaks down the sky and the whole earth seemed shaken by the thunder, I shouted and sang at the top of my voice. In this rushing wind, screaming past my ears, I was entering the eagle's world, the realm of the diving falcon.

It was dark when I reached home—a violent and ill-tempered dark filled with the crash of thunder and the lurid glare of lightning. Gramp was going about his chores with a lantern and Gram had the lamps lit and supper cooking on the kitchen stove. I changed to dry clothes and, exhilarated and happy, sat down to the simple and filling fare of cornmeal mush and milk.

With the thunder still muttering in the distance, that night, I went to bed—after telling in detail all the great adventures of the day. The next morning I set to work with redoubled effort on the machine which I hoped would carry me, too, aloft on man-made wings. When the following week's *Aero and Hydro* arrived, it contained a description of the events I had seen. "Soon after Havens' arrival at Michigan City," the account stated, "the storm broke and did its best to reduce the Curtiss flying boat to kindling wood. But ready helpers held the boat on the sands." As one of those ready helpers, I reflected, I had actually played a part in the world's first air-and-water marathon.

On succeeding days, while I tinkered with *The Dragonette,* I followed the progress of the Round-the-Great-Lakes competition with absorbing interest. When the Havens boat flashed across the finish line, winner of the 900-mile race, I felt I had had a part in the achievement. It seemed a good augury for the success of *The Dragonette.*

·16·

THE DRAGONETTE

ALL during the early weeks of the summer when I had just turned thirteen, I was engrossed in my great undertaking. Whenever the cracker-wagon rolled into the yard after a trip to town, slender sticks of spruce and white pine thrust out to the rear and bobbed up and down as the vehicle came to a stop. They were the raw material for the skeleton of *The Dragonette*.

Hour after hour I used to hammer and chisel away at thick pieces of galvanized sheet-iron, turning them into various fittings. Hour after hour I planed and sandpapered struts of spruce to give them a streamlined cross-section. I poured boiling water into a plugged iron pipe and then inserted five-foot sticks, half an inch square, to soften them for shaping the ribs. I cut piano wire into just the right lengths. And, as the weeks went by, an elaborate framework began to take shape under the old wagon-shed.

The curiosity of the cows increased daily. I was forced to put up two-by-four bars across the open front of the three-sided building. Then, for hours on end, the animals would stand with their heads thrust over the bars, chewing their cuds in sad-eyed contemplation.

In my own absorption I forgot about the woods and traps and animals. The only wild creatures I watched were my beloved swallows. As my eyes followed their sure evolutions I rode with them on imaginary flights of my own. When they were out of sight I would stop, from time to time, to pore over the pictures of real bird-men navigating the sky. In tattered copies of *Aircraft Magazine* and in the books which I carried home from the Michigan City Library there were thrilling and entrancing photographs which fed my imagination. I looked at some of them so many hundred times that they are still vivid in my mind. The most memorable were pictures which dramatized the beauty of flight and the moods of nature.

One, I recall, showed an exquisitively beautiful Hanriot monoplane flying at sunset; another depicted a wide-winged Antoinette, with its skiff-like body, banking around a pylon with a cloud-filled sky in the background; a third showed a "cross-channel type" Blériot rising over the ox-drawn cart of a peasant working in the fields of southern France; a fourth recorded Wilbur Wright riding through the air over a flock of sheep at sunset with the ruins of Rome in the background. During later years that picture, returning vividly to mind, became associated in mood with Robert Browning's lines:

> "Where the quiet-colored end of evening smiles,
> Miles and miles
> On the solitary pastures where our sheep
> Half-asleep
> Tinkle homeward thro' the twilight, stray or stop
> As they crop—
> Was the site once of a city great and gay. . . ."

There were, too, pictures of flying machines in the Webster's dictionary which had been installed on a spring-stand in the parlor. They showed the balloons, dirigibles, and heavier-than-air machines of the day. I looked longest at the dragonfly-like Antoinette and at Santos-Dumont's diminutive Demoiselle—a tiny, temperamental machine which early aviation writers referred to as "an infuriated grasshopper." So many times did I open the great book to this place that it began to fall open to the page whenever I spread apart the holding springs.

Balloons, at first, attracted me strongly. The stories of Blanchard, Wise, Santos-Dumont, Augustus Post, and Cromwell Dixon—a ten-year-old boy of Columbus, Ohio, who flew in a gas-bag his mother had sewed together on her sewing machine—provided vicarious thrills.

So long, and so intently, did I dream of aerial voyages that a mental adventure took place one day which I have never forgotten.

It was a still, hot Sunday afternoon. Gramp and I were sitting on the small hothouse frames which had been set up that spring just under the kitchen windows. The flies droned; the far-away whistle of a locomotive came faintly to my ears. We were silent in the heat. I was thinking of balloon-voyages through space, of drifting through the blue upper air, of viewing spread out below me the dunes, the marshes, the far hills of the Valparaiso moraine. Then, as vivid as reality, I saw a balloon drifting overhead, the passengers leaning over the side of the wicker basket and waving, the guide-rope dangling down in a thin line and trailing along the earth. All the while I knew no balloon was there. Yet the mental mirage was as clear as actuality.

My ambitions in the realm of lighter-than-air craft ended with a trip to Valparaiso. As the stellar attraction at a carnival there, a balloonist was scheduled to make a parachute jump. I pedaled my bicycle over twenty miles of gravel road—through the air that was filled, each time an auto passed, with choking white dust—to reach the place on the appointed day. The sooty canvas bag of the hot-air balloon was spread out on the bricks of a roped-off intersection near the center of town. A crowd was already pushing against the ropes.

Within the open space a short man with a head almost as square as a block of wood was sitting on a bicycle, a pad and pencil in hand, questioning a slender young man in his shirtsleeves. The little man's toes were pointed downward. His legs were just too short to reach the ground and, successively, the bicycle tipped off balance first to one side and then to the other. Each time, the rider gave an upward kick as his toe encountered the ground and the bicycle reared over in the opposite direction. Without being disturbed in the least by this seesawing through the air from side to side, the little man scribbled away at a furious rate. He was the local editor interviewing the daring aeronaut.

The interview was proceeding at a swift pace. The editor had just discovered that the aeronaut intended to marry a Valparaiso girl and settle down in the community. Like the occupant of a rowboat rushing downstream in the grip of a strong current, the interviewer kept to the main channel by dabbing in a question from time to time in the manner of giving a quick thrust with an oar. When the interview was over, the young man and a helper began preparing for the afternoon ascent. They called for volunteers to hold down the bag. I was one of the first through the ropes. With petroleum-fed flames heating the air within, the sooty bag rose slowly, bulged upward, assumed a pear-shaped form, tugged at our restraining hands.

At this critical moment some of the boys on the other side of the balloon let go. The great bag heeled over in our direction. There were shouts, clamor. We all let go and scattered. As I turned, I saw the bag gain upward momentum. The young man, now resplendent in blue tights, leaped for the trapeze bar. At the sudden jerk of his weight, the whole parachute pulled loose and he plunged back half a dozen feet to the hard surface of the pavement.

The unmanned balloon shot upward. It swung from side to side like the head of an angry elephant. A thousand feet in the air, it capsized and with black smoke pouring from the interior it drifted away, gradually sinking back to earth.

"If I can get *MEN* to hold the balloon"—the young man in the blue tights was shouting—"if I can get *MEN* to hold the balloon, I will make an ascent at seven o'clock tonight. But I will have to have *MEN* to do it!"

I wiped the soot off my hands on my trousers and wormed my way back into the crowd. Late that afternoon, as I was trundling my bicycle down a main street, I encountered a newsboy selling papers. I bought one and part way home stopped to rest under a tree and to read all about the aeronaut who was going to marry a Valparaiso girl and settle down in the community. That day brought my first encounter with the speed of the modern press and my last with hot-air ballooning.

After I had settled down to heavier-than-air machines I began collecting free catalogues. On post cards I wrote for booklets and price lists to all the fabulous advertisers in *Aircraft Magazine*. Back came catalogues on Curtiss biplanes, Paragon propellers, Gnome revolving motors. Each became a sort of Union Depot for dreams; imaginary journeys spread away from every page of these well-thumbed catalogues.

By the time I was eleven the number of model machines I had formed from whittled sticks of white pine, soft gray baling wire, and paper held in place by flour-and-water paste had reached the grand total of more than 120. With them I re-enacted in miniature all the historic events in the annals of flight, all the great aerial duels of the early days: Blériot and Latham vying for the honor and money accorded to the first to cross the English Channel; André Beaumont and Roland Garros battling neck and neck in the Paris-Rome race; J. Armstrong Drexel and Ralph Johnstone in a monoplane-versus-biplane struggle for supremacy in the upper air.

Among the entries in that entrancing catch-all at the back of *Vehicles of the Air*—the section headed "Tabular History of Flights"—I used to note such items as: "Flew in all directions," "Short flight, rudder broke," "Ninety feet high," "Passenger weighed 238 pounds," and "After only six and a half hours' instruction." Then, during lulls in my work on *The Dragonette*, I would reproduce these early adventures along the road of air-travel, using models of the pioneer machines involved.

On the previous Fourth of July one of my models had participated in a spectacular and almost disastrous rise and fall over the farm buildings. It was a lightweight eighteen-inch model of a Montgomery tandem glider. This I planned to send aloft secured to a Fourth-of-July paper balloon by means of a long fuse. When the fuse burned out, the glider would be cut loose automatically to spiral and volplane back to earth.

The Fourth was windy. Gramp helped me hold the balloon and light the paraffin-soaked excelsior ball which formed the heating plant of the tissue-paper craft. To be out of the gusts, we worked in the shelter of the wagon-shed. The brightly colored balloon expanded with the heated air. It tugged in my hands. I touched off the fuse and let go. Upward shot the bag, the glider dangling beneath. A gust from over the barn struck the balloon; it swayed violently from side to side. At a height of 100 feet its oscillations increased. Flames from the burning excelsior touched the tissue-paper and in a sudden swift flash of fire the whole balloon burned in mid-air. The glider model and the ball of burning excelsior plunged to earth only a few yards from the barn itself. That was—by request—the last experiment of the kind I made.

From models I graduated to man-carrying kites. One huge box kite, nearly ten feet long, was smashed in the launching, much to Gram's relief. Next came a small wing wired beneath the top bar of my bicycle. Pedaling like mad down a small decline, I would strike a "landing stage," formed by a plank running up on a box to produce a sort of miniature ski jump, and would go hurtling through the air for ten or a dozen feet before striking the earth again. On innumerable occasions the big red and white wagon-umbrella, with advertising slogans for Steiger's Hardware stenciled on the cloth, acted as a parachute in leaps from the upper beams of the big barn into the soft landing fields of the haymow. But best of all, and nearest to flying, was the dive and skim and zoom of the swing beneath the green shade of the lone oak.

By such stages I finally reached a tandem man-carrying glider. It had eighteen-foot wings and was designed somewhat after Samuel P. Langley's ill-fated machine. After short runs down the sloping roof of the chicken-coop I would launch myself on the mercies of the unsubstantial air. The word which best describes the result is a short, onomatopoetic one: Thump!

After such adventures, Gramp was wont to recite portions of Trowbridge's *Darius Green and His Flying Machine,* a large part of which he knew by heart. The lines which invariably seemed most appropriate were the final words of the poem:

> ". . . if you insist, as you have the right,
> On spreading your wings for a loftier flight,
> The moral is— Take care how you light."

All previous experiments were minor affairs compared to the building of *The Dragonette.* I had carefully planned out every detail. The streamlined body, covered with cloth, was fifteen feet long; the top wings had a spread of twenty-four feet and a width of five feet; the combined areas of the supporting surfaces were 220 square feet while the total weight of the machine was about 190 pounds. In lieu of a motor, I intended to have Dolly, Gramp's carriage horse, pull the machine at the end of a rope into the teeth of a stiff wind.

By late July the machine was taking shape. Under the

wagonshed the framework was resting in a series of assembled parts. Stove-bolts held the spruce and white pine sticks together and piano wire strengthened the various sections. When the skeleton of the fuselage had been equipped with a double pair of V-struts, holding the two coaster-wagon wheels of the landing gear, the time for covering the machine had arrived. Stretching heavy muslin taut, I anchored it in place with carpet-tacks. Similarly I covered the wings.

Stopping to watch me as he passed by, Gramp recalled other lines from Darius:

> "So day after day
> He stitched and tinkered and hammered away,
> Till at last 't was done—
> The greatest invention under the sun!
> 'An' now,' says Darius, 'Hooray fer some fun!' "

When all the cloth was on, Gram made up a huge dishpan full of hot starch. Using a whitewash brush, I set to work to coat the wings and fuselage with a sizing of starch which would make the fabric taut and more impervious to the air. By filling up the tiny openings in the muslin, I had decided, I could increase the lifting power of the wings.

On the side of the fuselage, in black paint, I labeled: *The Dragonette.* This sounded like my admired Antoinette and meant, in French,—I had deduced from my aeronautical books—"The Little Dragon." When this paint was dry I bolted the wings in place. Gramp, with additional quotations from Darius Green—such as "What's he got on? I van, it's wings! An' that 't other thing? I vum, it's a tail!"—held up the planes while I attached the bracing wires.

The finishing tuning-up brought the biggest thrill of all. This included tightening a dozen or more steel turnbuckles, just like those used on real airplanes. They had cost ten cents apiece and had come a few days before in a heavy brown pasteboard box from The Heath Aerial Vehicle Company, in Chicago. Several days of concentrated cherry-picking had gone into their purchase price.

My heart swelled until I could hardly breathe when I stood back and surveyed the wide-winged machine, poised and gleaming like a great white gull beneath the wagonshed. A neighbor had come over to see Gramp about borrowing his horse-rake. As he passed the wagonshed, he stopped in amazement.

"Thunderation, Ed! What's that?" he asked.

"It belongs to Darius Green, here," Gramp told him.

The man stared at the white contraption for a long time in silence. He walked around it. He examined it carefully. He peered into the cockpit. He thumped the starched muslin of the wings. Then he stood back, shook his head, and said with simple finality:

"*That* won't *never* fly!"

I said nothing. But in that moment with what intensity I wanted it to fly. I wanted to see him proved wrong. I wanted to laugh last just as the Wrights had laughed at their scoffers, just as Bell had done, just as Edison had done. With what poignancy the very young desire success! All life seems hanging on the brink; all the future seems decided by a yes or no. In later life we learn to discount our hopes, to expect a certain percentage of failures, struggle as we will. But in youth the world seems to remain solid, or dissolve around us, on the cast of a single die. Well, he was—in a way—proved wrong and that was consolation later on.

Haying was long over and Gramp had promised to tow *The Dragonette* across the lower forty if the wind was right on the following day. Before bedtime, that night, I walked out to the barnyard for a last glimpse of the white machine standing still in the moonlight with the velvet-black shadows of the wagonshed behind it. The stars were gleaming from a cloudless sky. Fair weather seemed assured for the great day, which now lay less than ten hours off.

·17·

A HOOSIER DARIUS GREEN

THE next morning I was pulling on my clothes at dawn. Outside the sky was clear and the thin green spire of the cedar tree was waving back and forth in a fresh breeze from the south. At a dog-trot I brought in kindling and wood and started the fire in the kitchen range. I hovered about the barn, urging Gramp on to greater speed in the milking. He sent me off to feed the horses.

At Dolly's stall I paused for a long contemplation and some misgivings. As she munched hay steadily at a low-gear pace, she had little resemblance to a compact and powerful motor. Her three distinguishing characteristics were a sweet and placid disposition, the largest feet I ever saw on a horse, and a little wornout tail that resembled a discarded whisk-broom. In the heyday of her turf career she may have attained a speed of twelve miles an hour.

My plan was simple. If this one-horsepower motor could pull *The Dragonette* at ten miles an hour into a twenty-five-mile-an-hour wind, the wings would have the same lifting capacity as though the machine were running over the ground at thirty-five miles an hour in a calm. This speed was the cue for *The Dragonette* to soar gracefully aloft.

It seemed weeks before the smell of coffee and bacon filled the kitchen. Then, when we sat down to steaming bowls of oatmeal and plates of fried eggs and bacon, Gramp developed an abnormal appetite. He ate endlessly. He asked for second helpings of everything. I wandered out to the wagonshed. The cows were draped over the bars as usual. I shooed them away and began to take down the two-by-fours which had protected *The Dragonette* from their curiosity.

For fully half an hour I tightened bolts, strummed wires, tested the controls. Still Gramp failed to put in an appearance. When he did come, he was not alone. My mother and father had appeared miraculously on the scene. Warned of the trend of events, they had arrived by an early train and had walked down from Furnessville.

While I waggled the control-stick, to show how the ailerons and elevator planes operated, and dilated upon the safety features of the big machine, Gramp harnessed Dolly. Then we set off in a procession for the lower meadow. At the head, the big feet of the carriage horse sent up little puffs of dust each time they plopped into the soft sand of the barnyard path. A long rope, used in pulling hay into the mow, trailed behind Dolly, attached to the whippletree. *The Dragonette* trundled along on her two wheels while I lifted the tail and my mother and father each grasped a wing-tip. Gram, filled with doubts as to the wisdom of the whole procedure, brought up the rear.

At the lower bars, where I had so often watched the Lone Oak swallows, there was a short pause. The machine had to be lifted over as the passage was not wide enough to accommodate the twenty-four-foot wings of the biplane. When he built those bars, Gramp remarked, he never thought *flying machines* would have to go through them!

As we trooped into the wide open spaces of the hayfield, the breeze had freshened until the leaves of a near-by oak tree were fluttering in the wind. My mother and father explained that they intended to run along at the ends of the wings to hold me down if I began to climb into too rarefied an atmosphere. On this information, I designated them "the wing mechanics." Gramp remained "the head mechanician."

Dolly sidled past *The Dragonette* with the whites of her eyes showing and the long hay-rope was tied securely to the axle of the biplane. At this point an interruption occurred. I heard a scraping sound at the tail of the machine. An inquisitive calf had followed us through the gate and was licking the starch off one of the elevator planes. Starch, to that calf, was what catnip is to cats. Every time I would chase it away, it would gallop, tail-high, in a wide circle and reappear on the other side of *The Dragonette.* Fully ten minues were spent rushing this way and that before the animal was outside the field and the gate securely locked.

With my cap turned around backwards and a pair of goggles in place, I prepared to climb into the cockpit. There was a last-minute inspection of the turnbuckles and bolts, the elevator hinges, and the control-wires. Then I settled myself down on the seat of crisscrossing laths and grasped the control-stick. My head was just sticking above the top of the deep-chested, covered-in fuselage. On either hand the wide, white wings stretched away—ending in my father on one side and my mother on the other. For an instant pictures of splintered planes and dead little boys kaleidoscoped before my mind. Then I noticed my mother was looking white and scared. Paradoxically, that cheered me up.

I lifted my right hand high above my head. I had seen André Beaumont doing that in a picture taken at the start of the Paris-Rome race. It was the signal for the take-off.

A hundred feet or so out in front, the head mechanician turned over the motor—or, rather, turned it around, because by this time Dolly had become tangled in the rope and traces and had to be untangled. When this was accomplished, and the horse was headed directly into the wind, Gramp clucked loudly.

Nothing happened.

He shouted: "Git ap, confound you!"

The horse remained rooted in place.

Gramp slapped the lines over her bony back. Still she remained unmoving. Looking wall-eyed, she glanced apprehensively back at the white machine. She gave her worn-out, whisk-broom tail a few nervous jerks. Seemingly she was overwhelmed by the great role she was about to play in the conquest of the air.

Then, without warning—when we least expected it—she charged ahead, broke into a run, then a gallop. Gramp galloped behind her. My mother and father galloped beside the wings. Gramp's hat blew off and his beard trailed in the wind. I was so taken by surprise that I forgot to operate the controls. We bumped for a hundred yards and then rolled to a stop. There was silence. Nobody had any breath to say anything with except the aviator who had forgotten to ascend and he had nothing to say. I clambered out and, lifting the tail, swung *The Dragonette* around. Slowly we trailed back up the field to the starting point.

After a ten-minute rest under the oak tree, we took our places again. I wet my finger and held it aloft. The wind had veered a little to the east. It seemed dying out. Hurriedly Gramp got Dolly in motion and once more we went careening down the field. I could see the two wing-mechanics preparing to cling to the machine if it began to rise. Cautiously I inched back the control-stick. Nothing happened. I pulled the stick clear back in my lap. The same result. Now we were slowing down at the end of the run. I felt discouraged as I scrambled out. The wind was coming in fits and starts. The steady, strong breeze of the morning was gone.

On the third run down the field I noticed my father was lifting up on his wing instead of holding it down. And on the fourth attempt he said he was positive he could hold the machine down and keep it from going *too* high all by himself. So we left my mother fanning herself in the shade of the oak tree. It was during this trip that everything seemed to happen at once.

Dolly, towing Gramp at the end of the reins and towing *The Dragonette* at the end of the hay-rope, got away for a fast start. My father raced along, tugging upward on his wing-tip as though in an effort to heave the flying machine into the air by main force. A strong rush of wind whistled among the wires and pounded along the taut, starched muslin. As the gust struck the wide-spread wings, there was a sudden lift. The bumping stopped.

My father shouted feebly: "You're flying!"

Then he tripped and disappeared.

The gust also left us and the wheels of *The Dragonette* struck the ground. One landed in a rut. The machine slewed wildly to the right. A wing-tip dug into the earth. There was a splintering crash and the sharp report of a snapping strut. The plane heeled over, plowed along on its nose, and came to a stop. A cloud of fine gray dust was settling through the air when I crawled out and looked around. My father was picking himself up from the floor of the pasture. Gram and my mother were running in my direction from the oak tree. Entirely unharmed, I began to bewail the fate of my machine.

Then I noticed that Gramp didn't seem happy either. He was hopping around one one leg, holding the other. His face was screwed up until all I could see was whiskers. From time to time a red hole would appear among the whiskers and out would come loud and violent affirmations of anguish. In answer to my questions I learned, in exclamatory and disconnected sentences, what had happened.

The sudden jerk on the hay-rope, when the machine slewed around, had thrown the whippletree violently to one side. It had struck Gramp squarely on the shin. As he unhitched Dolly and limped off to apply Sloan's liniment to the bruise, he resigned as my head mechanician. In fact he severed all connection with future aerial experimentation forever.

I walked disconsolately around and around the shattered *Dragonette*. Gram and my mother offered comforting words and then started for the house to get dinner. My father told me how he had seen the wheels lift from the ground and the machine go sailing like a great kite into the air. An extremely truthful man, he held in his imagination with a tight rein. He couldn't say how high the machine had risen. Even under pressure he would only say that the wheels had not risen *more* than five feet in the air. Of that he was sure.

He, too, started for the house and, like Gray's departing plowman, left the world to darkness and to me. My gloom lifted slightly when I reflected that, in spite of everything, I had—for a few moments—ridden on wings through that magical realm of the air. I examined *The Dragonette* more carefully, taking an inventory of the sound and damaged parts. Only one lower wing and the landing gear had been completely demolished. The rest of the machine was virtually intact. A couple of week's work under the wagonshed would repair the damage. But before that work could be begun an unforeseen event made the catastrophe complete.

After supper that night I walked down to the pasture where, with one white wing thrust upward, *The Dragonette* lay beneath the sunset sky. The west had an angry look and I drove half a dozen stakes into the hard, dry ground and attached ropes to anchor down the machine in the event of a storm. This was a wise precaution, but the protection was insufficient.

Late that night I awoke to the sound of gust-driven rain, crashing thunder, and wind that lashed the great oak with a sound like booming surf. Battering down fields of standing corn, tearing away branches from trees, the most violent thunderstorm of a stormy year continued hour after hour.

Under the broken sky of early morning I hurried through the dripping grass to the south forty. Strewn half-way across the field were fragments of *The Dragonette*. It had torn loose from its moorings and had rolled like a tumbleweed before the great gusts. Its twenty-four-foot wings, its streamlined fuselage, its tail-surfaces were kindling wood and shreds of cloth and snarls of wire.

With that catastrophe of wind and storm my attempts to be a pioneer of the air came to an end. Gramp's cows returned with untroubled minds to their grazing. The wagonshed once more became a wagonshed. Dolly went back to the staid orbit of her former days. And I plunged once again into the green world and the long-neglected enchantments of the out-of-doors.

·18·

WINTERGREEN BERRIES

ON A recent day, a thousand miles from Lone Oak, I came upon a little patch of woodland moss. From its soft, green embrace a dozen low plants lifted pointed leaves and round crimson berries. At the sight, somewhere back among the sleeping memories of my brain one stirred, stretched, and became awake.

It was the memory of a September day. Vacation at Lone Oak was nearing its end. The gentle melancholy which hung like an Indian summer haze over these latter days of freedom colored my emotions. Alone I wandered along the winding paths of the north woods. Cicadas shrilled in the oaks and catbirds and brown thrashers darted in and out among the tangled underbrush. Near the wood's northern boundary a small spring welled out of the moss and saturated the soil of a depression. Running away up the slopes of this hollow among the trees was the green plush carpet of the moss and sprinkled over it was a crimson profusion of wintergreen berries.

Never since have I seen them so numerous, so large, so filled with flavor. Stretched out on the moss of the cool glade, I found hundreds of the berries within reach of my fingers. I filled my hands and lay back at leisure munching the firm white meat and savoring to the full the wild flavor of the wintergreen fruit. Coleridge has the lines: "For he on honey-dew hath fed and drunk the milk of Paradise." Worthy of a place with these magical foods are the wintergreen berries of a northern wood.

From early days wintergreen was a flavor that gave me my greatest delight. At the ornate Canditorium, on Main Street in Michigan City, I used to reach a seventh heaven and enter in when a wintergreen soda, with coral-pink foam, was set before me. At that time Jumbo gum was to be had in the local stores. It supplied the most gum possible for five cents. Each stick was nearly a quarter of an inch thick and permeating its delectable depths was the flavor of wintergreen.

My progress through the world, in later years, has been something of an Odyssey in search of wintergreen sodas and Jumbo gum. In each new town I have visited, on both coasts and in between, I have looked hopefully on soda-fountain menus and candy counters for these delights of boyhood. And all in vain. As far as I can find out, wintergreen sodas were a specialty of the Canditorium and Jumbo gum was indigenous to the region.

There was another gum, a wild gum, that was free for the taking in one section of the Lone Oak woods. This was the pitch of the spruce trees. It oozed out in shining globules which slowly hardened on contact with the air. I called the cluster of spruces "The Chewing-Gum Trees." The rich, spicy flavor of the globules had a slightly bitter tang and I remember that the consistency of the pitch had to be just right or it stuck to my teeth with the grip of glue.

Other treasures besides wintergreen berries and spruce gum lay in the north woods. It, like the dunes farther to the north, was a stronghold of the wild amid the tameness of advancing civilization. Cottontails lived under the old brushpiles and made their runways through the undergrowth. Bushes and trees sheltered the nests of many birds. And, here and there, my eye caught the exciting, half-hidden entrances to the dens of the burrowing animals. Moving silently down the narrow trails, I would come upon little open glades which looked wild and lonely as though in Indian days. The home-life of baby birds and young squirrels and infant rabbits formed only one of the manifold chapters unfolded before me in this book of the woods.

Gram understood best of all the fascination of this wooded tract. To Gramp the north woods was largely a source of firewood and fence-posts. He belonged to a generation such as the Psalmist described, one in which "a man was famous according as he had lifted up axes upon the thick trees." In earlier days Gramp had earned his living, during winter months, by chopping down trees as a woodsman and cutting them into stovewood at so much a cord. When he was long past sixty he was still seemingly tireless in his expert use of an ax.

Whenever he started off on a chopping expedition to the north woods I tagged at his heels. Sometimes we would carry sandwiches of home-baked bread and thick slices of boiled beef and Gramp would stop work at noontime—or a little before—and we would seek out the spring in the little glade and dine in state on its spreading carpet of moss or on a fallen log near by.

The trees that came crashing down beneath his sturdy strokes always had stories to tell. One would have a flicker hole for me to investigate; another, loose bark with its population of small inhabitants beneath. Once the fall of an oak stunned a red squirrel which had taken refuge in its massed nest of leaves. While Gramp worked, I used to chew the twig-tips of sassafras or ruminate on wintergreen leaves or build brush igloos with the branches which had been lopped from the trunks of fallen trees.

There was, on the far western outskirts of the woods, a spot which is associated in my mind with both food and adventure. Running wild over a considerable area, blackberry bushes spread out in a seemingly impenetrable tangle. As the summer days advanced, and the fruit hung thick upon this bramble-patch, Gramp and Gram and I would organize an expedition.

In preparation for such forays Gram would tie her blue sunbonnet firmly on her head and we all would arm ourselves with pails of varying sizes to hold the wild harvest we were after. The start was usually made in mid-morning after the sun had dried the dew but before the peak heat of the day had come. Arriving at the patch, we would skirt the bramble thicket, picking the outer berries first.

It was after this initial skimming along the edges was over that the real fun began.

Gramp was trailbreaker. He would flounder through the briers, stamping them down with his heavy shoes and we would follow in his wake, picking the blackberries to right and left. As he worked deeper into the tangle he would report his progress from time to time.

"Come over here," he would call, "th' berries are thicker'n thieves."

Once, when an interlaced thicket of brambles defied all his efforts at penetration, he burst out:

"Nothin' but a greased pig with his ears pinned back could git through that tangle!"

Oftentimes the briers rose far higher than my head. I used to peer into the brambly depths of the vegetation on either side of the path Gramp had made, forgetting all about picking until Gram overtook me or Gramp glanced back and brought me to life with some comment on my lack of industry such as:

"Edwin, 'ts too bad y' weren't born rich 'stead o' handsome!"

The trails opened up virgin wilderness on a minute scale. They carried me into the depths of a realm previously hidden from sight by a living wall of vegetation. Peering among the briers, I could see abandoned bird's nests and rabbit runways. Like disengaged bits of twigs, walking-stick insects—green and brown—moved away over the foliage. And those living leaves, the katydids, lifted their veined, green wings and swung their thread-like antennae up and down and from side to side, exploring the suddenly disrupted world around them.

Behind me I could hear the steady patter of blackberries dropping into the large tin pail that Gram carried. I had a smaller lard pail which had been scrubbed and scalded for the occasion. Into this receptacle I would pick rapidly for several minutes. Then some new sight of small wild-life activity would absorb me. Gram understood without explanations and said nothing about these sudden lapses of mine.

At intervals she would inquire of Gramp: "Don't you think you have got enough paths? Hadn't you better stop and pick a while?"

But Gramp always had just one more trail to make. Beyond was better. He would pause and pick a few dozen berries, then wander on in search of a place where they were thicker. He was the pioneer spirit in action. He had implicit faith that better picking lay somewhere just ahead. Sometimes he was right. But when the expedition was over it was Gram who had filled most of the pails.

As noon approached, Gramp would squint up at the sun and then pull out his big gold watch.

"Mother," he would say, "these berries are gettin' t' be small 'taters an' a few t' a hill. 'Ts almost noon an' 'ts hotter'n all git out. Let's go home."

As we walked back across the fields for dinner, Gramp would view the gallons of fresh fruit, which the winter would see appearing from glass cans to provide a welcome dessert, and remark complacently:

"Well, we picked a good lot o' berries t'day, didn't we?"

And Gram would say:

"Yes, *we* killed the bear!"

And we all would laugh.

·19·

BEYOND THE DUNES

"KEEP yer eye peeled fer fun!"

When Gramp had said that at milking time, I knew something special was in the air. A little later he let me in on the secret. We were going to the lake. Once or twice a summer, on the Fourth of July or during a lull after haying or when all the daughters of the family were home, we packed a picnic lunch and made an expedition to the dunes.

As the sandhill crane flew, the distance from Lone Oak to the lake was hardly a mile and a half. Even by the roundabout road we took, it was a journey of less than three miles. Yet a trip to Lake Michigan was a gala event that required days of preparation.

Long in advance, Gramp would pick out the best chickens for frying. On the day preceding the trip the kitchen would be filled with the aroma of baking bread. The sound of the egg-beater would carry out into the yard as Gram prepared the mystic ingredients for angel food and No Name cake. That evening, after supper was over, more wood was stoked into the kitchen range and the whole house became redolent with the smell of frying chicken. I was packed off to bed early to get extra sleep for the big day ahead—and also to get me out from underfoot in the kitchen.

Lying under the low ceiling in the little room at the head of the stairs, I would breathe deeply of the delicious kitchen-smells and wriggle with delight at the prospects of the morrow.

We were all up at dawn. Gramp milked at double-speed while I put in an extra ration of oats for the horses. We hurried through a pick-up breakfast. Then, while Gramp harnessed Deck and Colty to the haywagon, the dinner was stowed away in baskets. Gram made a final inventory—chicken, bread, butter, sandwiches, deviled eggs, potato salad, cakes, lemonade, pickles. All were present and accounted for. The baskets were swung into the center of the hayrack and covered with cloths to keep out the dust. We climbed aboard. Gramp clucked to the horses and away down the road we rolled, our legs dangling over the side of the hayrack and a cloud of dust behind us settling down on the wayside plants.

Our course led east along the sand-road, then north down Schrum's Hill—where huge inch-grass lifted straight green spikes from a ditch-side—and finally, after crossing the Michigan Central tracks and driving west a few rods on what is now the Dunes Highway, north again over a narrow corduroy road formed of logs laid side by side on the uncertain footing of the bog. So spongy was the foundation of this makeshift road that our passing wheels produced a miniature earthquake in the swamp. Water in the ditches at either side would quiver and plants growing on the opposite banks would tremble as though in a breeze.

At the far side of the swamp-belt the horses climbed upward. They labored in the deep sand of a winding road, a road that carried us past a solitary dwelling set amid pine trees. It was the only habitation in all that lonely stretch of dunes. In it lived unusual people who will be mentioned later in this chapter. Beyond the house the road swept in wide curves among the sandhills and then plunged down a decline of soft sand to the unfrequented beach which was our destination.

By a sense of smell alone I could have followed our progress on that journey. First came the odor of hot, dry dust; then the heavy, acrid smell of the swamp; then the penetrating, unforgettable aroma of the duneland pines; and finally that stirring freshness, the breath of the great inland lake.

I was usually some distance ahead of the horses when

we reached the descent to the shore. As far as I could see the beach stretched away, deserted and lonely, as unaltered by civilization as though man had never existed. My first concern was the water. Under my clothes I wore a woolen bathing suit inherited from my father. Behind me, as I raced across the hot sand, I left a trail of discarded garments. The water of the lake was always cool, even on the hottest days, and that first dip was a thing long to be remembered. It was like the first lick of an ice-cream cone, the first sip of a wintergreen soda, or the first swallow of lemonade after a long walk in dusty August.

Gramp usually went swimming in a pair of overalls. He plowed through the water with a determined, steady breaststroke, swimming "sailor-fashion" for alarming distances. When he reached the second sandbar we all would set up a shout for him to come back. But he would keep on, his head growing smaller and smaller, until finally we saw him stand up, a small figure, resting in the shallows of the third and outer bar.

Once, after his return to shore, he suddenly clapped his hand on an overall pocket.

"Jumpin' Jerusalem!" he ejaculated. "It's gone!"

"What's gone?" Gram asked.

"Th' money!"

"What money?"

"Th' sixty dollars!"

"What sixty dollars?"

"Y'know—th' sixty we got fer th' calves. I was afraid

't leave th' roll o' bills in th' house so I brought 'em along. Forgot all about 'em when I went swimmin'. They must o' washed out in th' water."

Sixty dollars was a great sum and we rushed about over the sand, and in the shallow water, but we searched in vain. After that, even though the bills were found miraculously washed up on the sand the following morning, we had no more trouble with Gramp swimming too far from shore. He confined himself to the shallow water and rarely ventured beyond the sandbar that was nearest to the beach.

As noon approached Gram would start spreading out blankets in the shade of a large pine tree. On a tablecloth in the middle there would appear a mouthwatering array. I would be given the job of shooing flies away and as a recompense I was permitted to sample, surreptitiously, a chicken wing or a bit of frosting. As soon as everything was in place, and Gram gave the word, I would dash away to round up the clan. Like a sheep-dog harrying a wayward flock, I would urge on the loiterers.

In a ring around the central tablecloth we would attack the mounds of fried chicken, the thick, light slices of new bread, the piles of sandwiches, the clusters of deviled eggs, the angel food cakes and the buckets of lemonade. Sometimes there would be a freezer of homemade ice cream, yellow-rich with cream and eggs. At other times watermelons would be kept packed in ice until Gramp got out his big, bone-handled jackknife, wiped it ceremoniously on his overalls, and began cutting the great crisp, juicy slices, sugar-sweet.

After dinner, while the older folk sat in the shade or snoozed with their hats lying over their faces to keep away the flies, I often wandered alone along the deserted beach. Sometimes I would walk for miles. White gulls would lift from the shore ahead of me and go skimming away over the water. Crows would rise from some feast, where a fish was stranded, flapping away to duneside pines. Their raucous cawing carried far through the hot silence. Across the water and along the beach there was no sign of human life. The waves of a vast deserted lake rolled on a lonely shore. It was thus that the Indians had seen the dune country—and the French explorers and the voyageurs and the earliest pioneers. Here, beyond the horizon of the yellow dunes, I entered, for a time, a glorious, primitive world of the past.

As I walked along the beach I tried to pick out the high dunes that I could see from my rooftop perch. And when I wandered about in one of the amphitheater-like blowouts which pierced the ridge of sandhills I would climb the farther edge and peer, with shaded eyes, out across the green prairies of the bog to the wooded hills and hollows beyond. Somewhere in that direction lay the clustered buildings and the giant tree of Lone Oak Farm.

On open spaces of clear sand, among the dunes, I would find traceries of beetles and centipedes, as delicate as lacework. Little lizards, called six-lined swifts, scuttled among the leaves and grass. Absorbed in such things, I would wander far. Then, suddenly, I would be overtaken by fears of becoming lost among the dunes and I would hurry back to the beach, which stretched away like an open road bordered by the dunes and the water.

On the way back I would loiter and zigzag, following the wave-marks on the wet sand, picking up treasures—corks from fishing nets, drowned insects, water-smoothed pebbles, and small and fragile shells. Occasionally I came upon the bony armor-plates of a dead sturgeon or a drowned bat or stranded timbers from some wrecked vessel. When I arrived with my treasure-trove back at the site of the picnic Gram would be packing the silverware into the baskets and Gramp would be fortifying himself with remnants of the feast before hitching the horses to the wagon.

We all would be more subdued on the way back. The heat of the day would lessen as the sun drew nearer the horizon and we would jolt along, relaxed and happy, as the horses headed for home. Oftentimes we stopped to pass the time of day with the Nicholsons, who lived in the house among the pines.

The father was superintendent of a huge area which had been purchased by a member of the Chicago Board of Trade, A. Stamford White, in the late Eighteen-Hundreds. Originally it comprised an area of 2,200 acres and stretched for five miles along the shore of the lake. Both the Palmers, the earliest caretakers living in the isolated farmhouse, and the Nicholsons, the occupants of a later day, were friends of my grandparents.

According to the story, the wilderness of dunes and swampland had been purchased with the idea of turning it into a summer resort. Grasses of various kinds were sent out to the Palmers and tested in an effort to anchor down the shifting yellow sand. None of them succeeded and the scheme was abandoned. Then cattle were established among the lush vegetation of the marshes. Rattlesnakes, striking the lowered noses of the feeding animals, made this project unprofitable. Hearing that some breeds of pigs are nearly immune to snakebite, the owner shipped out a herd of red porkers. They not only seemed unaffected by the snakes but sometimes killed and ate the reptiles. At times there would be hundreds of these red pigs fattening in pens for the packing houses.

By the time our horses swung around the bend by O'Keefe's woods and we saw the comforting sight of the great oak, rising black against the sunset sky, Gramp and I both were "as dry as chips and as hungry as wolves." The jolting had shaken us down and we were ready for more. We slaked our thirst on spring water and set about the chores.

While we fed the chickens and pigs and calves and Gramp milked the cows, Gram stirred golden cornmeal into boiling, salted water in an iron pot. She added two fresh eggs and beat the mixture steadily for three minutes. Then she covered the pot and set it on the back of the range for twenty minutes. Her own inimitable kind of cornmeal mush was ready.

Half an hour later, when twilight had fallen and we had finished our various tasks, we found bowls of mush and a pitcher of creamy milk awaiting us. On this simple fare we ended our day of adventure.

·20·

SMITH HILL

HIRED hands came and went at Lone Oak. Some were local men and some drifted into the circle of our lives and drifted out again almost like moths pausing in the light of a street-lamp and then winging their way out into the darkness beyond. We knew relatively little about many of them—their history or their destination. They became members of the family for the space of a harvest season; then they disappeared forever. A few lived on in memory through their eccentricities.

There was one giant of a man, a silent Swede about fifty years old, who had a mania for clean shirts. Two or three times a day he would disappear into the barn to reappear clad in a different shirt. In the evening we would see him down by the spring, washing his shirts and hanging them on the fence to dry. As I remember it, he seemed to have a single pair of trousers but an inexhaustible supply of shirts.

Another hired hand, who stayed for nearly a year, was a wiry little Irishman with an uptilted nose, a hot-potato-in-his-mouth brogue and the not-uncommon name of Pat. Pat had a tremendous capacity for excitement culminating in what appeared to be lapse of memory. When he was hoeing in one field and Gramp in another he would suddenly throw down his hoe as though he had just remembered something of life-and-death importance. He would run like mad across the fields, waving his arms and yelling:

"Mishter Way! *Mishter Way!* MISHTER WAY!"

Thinking the house was on fire or Pat had been bitten by a rattlesnake, Gramp would drop his hoe and run to meet him, shouting: "What is it, Pat?"

Pat would reach him breathless, stop, scratch his head, and say: "Oh, nuthin'."

Then he would plod silently back across the fields and resume his hoeing. Gramp could never quite make up his mind whether he was affected by the sun or was just getting a rest and relieving the monotony with synthetic excitement.

Of all the hired hands who received their dollar a day from Gramp the one I remember best is Smith Hill.

He was a large-framed man, six feet in height but so stooped and bowed that he seemed fully half a foot shorter. His face was, as Gramp put it, the color of a peeled potato. His silky, corn-tassel beard never attained a length of more than three inches. It had the same pale yellow hue as his hair. Eyes, which were unusually large and of the palest blue, looked out from beneath a brow, abnormally high and unmarred by a single wrinkle.

When he walked, Smith Hill seemed to be wearing snowshoes. He shuffled along with a slow, measured tread, his oversize shoes sliding along the surface of the ground. To insure against having his toes pinched, he always bought shoes several sizes too large. When the soles wore through he put on new soles himself, using carpet tacks and clinching over the points inside. Almost never were his shoes mates and frequently he would put in an appearance at the farm with one foot encased in a rubber boot and the other in a leather shoe.

As though to make up for the slowness of his gait, Smith took unusually long steps. Even so, more than an hour was consumed in plodding to Lone Oak from his cabin a mile and a half to the south. His activity throughout the day was equally deliberate. Nothing could spur him on to greater effort because, literally, he was going at top speed. For decades a simile current in the region was: As slow as Smith Hill.

Once Gramp found him picking up apples with one hand, his other hand resting comfortably in a capacious overall pocket. In the interests of increased production,

Gramp remarked that a neighboring farmer, in a similar situation, had once asked a hired man:

"How much would you charge for the use of your other hand?"

The barb missed the mark entirely. Smith Hill shook his head slowly and remarked with deliberate emphasis: "He always was an insultin' old feller, *wa'nt he?*"

In the midst of the potato harvest one summer, when we were busy picking up the crop, putting big potatoes in one bag and little potatoes in another, Gramp discovered that Smith had been dropping big and little potatoes in the same bag. He had him dump them out and sort them over. Smith remarked dryly:

"Wal, Ed, ef y' want t' pay me fer pickin' 'taters up an' dumpin' 'em out an' pickin' 'em up again, don't know as I orter care."

At the time of the Russo-Japanese War he took a great interest in the fortunes of the Russians. Each morning he would appear at the kitchen door with the same query: "What's the news about Rooshie?"

Gram, who always read the paper to Gramp while he lay on the couch and rested—or went to sleep—would summarize the events as given in the latest dispatches. She took a kindly interest in Smith and often at the end of the day, when he was leaving, she would slip some fresh food into the battered tin lard pail in which he brought his lunch. Whenever she asked him if he would like something of the kind—some fresh Johnnycake, or meat, or cookies, or buttermilk—he would hesitate a minute and then remark: " 'T would come in handy."

During winter months, when he sometimes came over to help in sawing wood, he "sat in" for hot meals when noon arrived. He had peculiarities of his own in connection with mealtime. In spite of his old clothes he was fanatically clean. He would scrub and lather and snort and suds for an unconscionably long time while Gramp and I restrained ourselves with difficulty from attacking the fried pork and steaming boiled potatoes set out on the oilcloth-covered kitchen table.

Smith liked tea and soup boiling hot. He never drank tea from a cup. Invariably he poured a few tablespoonfuls into the saucer, swirled it around with slow dexterity to cool it to his taste and then gulped it down, smacking his lips loudly after each swallow. In the matter of soup, he scorned the smaller spoons. He wanted the largest one available. With such a utensil he would ladle out some of the boiling-hot fluid, then, holding the spoon as far from his lips as was practicable, he would suck the soup across the intervening space, cooling it in transit.

One blustery March day, after the meal was over and he and Gramp were sitting before the kitchen range storing up a little extra heat before going out into the piercing wind, Smith remarked out of a clear sky:

"Wal, Ed, so y' fin'ly got rich!"

Gramp laughed.

"I hadn't heard about it," he said.

"Y' own yer own place, don'tcha?"

"Well, yes."

"Y' got horses an' cows an' chickens, ain'tcha?"

"Yes."

"Y' got a rig t' ride in? Y' got a good wife an' good children? Y' take *two* newspapers, don'tcha?"

"Yes."

"Well, ef y' don't think yer rich now—when will y' be?"

In his younger days Smith lived in a one-room log cabin with his father, two brothers—Zack and Rufus, and a sister —Lavina. Early one Sunday morning a neighbor was driving past the cabin when a sudden hubbub broke out within. There were howls and screams and the sound of scuffling. Chairs were overturned and above the commotion Rufus was shouting at the top of his lungs:

"Shirt him, Pap, shirt him! I'll help!"

The neighbor hitched his horse and went in to investigate. He was met at the door by the breathless old man.

"Oh, it ain't nothin'," he explained. "Ever' Sunday we have t' git out th' pitchforks t' make Zack put on a clean shirt."

Smith's only sister, Lavina, eventually married a man named Clark and moved to a cabin near Burdick. Their only child was a daughter, named Jerushia. Life was far from easy for the family and after a dozen years the husband was killed, late one fall, in an accident. When Lavina was told the news, her first reaction was:

"Wal, wa'nt that just like him—t' go an' git hisself killed 'fore he banked up th' house fer th' winter!"

Later she and Jerushia made ends meet as best they

could. One time Gram stopped to see if Lavina wanted a ride to church.

"I'd like t' go, Mis' Way," she said, "I'd like t' go powerful well. But I kaint. Jerushy's got th' stockin's on."

For a dozen years, off and on, Smith Hill helped out as an "extra hand" at Lone Oak. As the years went by his movements became even slower. In exasperation Gramp would declare:

"Beside Smith a snail is a streak o' greased lightnin'. He's th' slowest man on th' face o' the earth, s' help me Thirty-Six!"

But there came a time when our years of joking turned to emotions of pity and regret. For the end of Smith Hill's handicapped days came in a singularly tragic manner. Caught in a blizzard, he was making his way home along the Michigan Central Railroad tracks when he was struck and killed by a through-express.

He had carefully chosen the left-hand track in order to face any train which might approach. But during the hours he was slowly plodding between the rails a tie-up occurred on the right-hand tracks. At Michigan City a dispatcher, in his lighted brick tower amid the storm, had shunted the fast express to the left-hand rails where Smith was walking. Thus the train, running on the wrong tracks, had come out of the snow behind him.

·21·

WAGONSHED MUSEUM

I HAD made a great discovery.

In the Field of the Serpents, north of Gramp's woods, the drifting of the sand had brought to light the bleached skeleton of a long-dead cow. Day after day I had returned to the spot, on the alert for wriggling serpents and stopping at frequent intervals to remove sandburrs from my bare feet. And day after day I had struggled home again laden with ribs and femurs, with bones from neck and tail.

In one corner of the wagonshed the pile of these trophies grew in size until the whole skeleton of the cow was there, with the white skull resting in a place of honor on top. The most spectacular exhibit of all had been added to my wagonshed museum.

That summer, while the mowing machines, cultivators, and horse-rakes were again out in the fields, I had taken possession of the long, low, black-tarpaper-covered structure. This time it was for the housing of a rapidly accumulating mass of arrowheads, birds' nests, oddly twisted sticks from the north woods, and other natural history odds and ends. Lettered on the cover of a strawberry crate and nailed to one of the uprights of the shed was the legend:

WAY-TEALE MUSEUM

The open front of the wagonshed faced the south; its back was to the north. Thus, during those driving winter blizzards which swept down over the Great Lakes out of the northwest, the low structure stood like some stoical old horse planted firmly with its back to the wind. Trampled earth formed the floor of the shed and the uprights were thick poles of sassafras. To some of these poles the ridged, rough bark still clung. On others it had been worn away and the wood beneath was polished where the cows had rubbed their necks on days when the flies were bad.

Along the back of this shed I had constructed a rising tier of narrow shelves. Gram let her dish-washing wait while she helped me arrange on two of these shelves the arrowheads, spearheads, and tomahawk-heads that I had picked up on The Island and in the fields at plowing time.

During one whole day I sawed limbs from a score or more of trees to get exhibits of bark and wood. There were rows of leaves and acorns from the great oak tree. There were wasp-nests and the masonry of the mud-daubers. Empty birds' nests had many shelves to themselves. In one day I collected fourteen kinds of birds' nests. The easiest to get were the mud bowls of the robins and the hair-lined nests of the chipping sparrows; the hardest, the dangling baskets of the orioles.

Queerly shaped roots were lined up along one wall. Discarded snakeskins dangled their translucent lengths above them. Stones of various sizes and shapes, colors and histories, terraced the foot of the opposite wall. Some of these stones, water-polished, came from the dunes, as did the fish skeletons, the drowned insects, and the bony armor-plating of the sturgeon. Small medicine bottles held different kinds of dirt and sand. And cheese boxes, nailed to various parts of the shed's interior, held a fearful and wonderful assortment of oddments.

Crayon-labeled bits of cardboard informed the casual visitor of the character and rarity of each exhibit. In this work the birds' nests and snakeskins were comparatively easy. But when I reached the mineralogical specimens I was stumped. Above the sloping pile of rocks I placed a single large sign reading: STONES.

My initial inscription over the pile of white bones, which had been transported with such great labor from the Field of the Serpents, stated simply: COW SKELETON. As time went on that seemed too drab a heading for this stellar attraction. So, after much thought, I changed it to read: BOVINE SKELETON.

On the packed-dirt floor of the shed I used to spend hours at a time trying to fit the bones together into a complete skeleton. I was like the proverbial boy with the dismantled watch; there were always some parts left over. After such fruitless efforts I would walk down near the spring, where Gramp's cows congregated under a tree. I would look at the animals with X-ray eyes, trying to fathom the mysteries of their bony structure. One mild-mannered milch-cow, which Gramp called Mooley, would stand patiently for minutes at a time while I ran my hand exploringly over her ribs, down her spine, and along her forelegs. In all probability, from her viewpoint, I was an extra moving tail and chased the flies away.

Little was learned from such investigations and eventually I gave up my efforts and arranged the bones in rows on either side of the weathered skull. Placed in a decreasing scale of size beyond were the skulls of a dog, a cat, a rabbit, a rat, and a mouse.

Hand-in-hand with this gathering of museum specimens another activity kept me absorbed. This was the jotting down of nature notes. W. H. Hudson, in one of his essays, refers to the process of putting down notes while walking afield as "picking up sticks." When you have enough sticks you can start a fire. When he had enough notes he could write an essay. Similarly Thomas Gray, of the classic *Elegy,* used to maintain that one note jotted down on the spot was worth a wagonload of reminiscences.

Before I was eight years old I was, without knowing it, following the precepts of Hudson and Gray. As I roamed the fields I scribbled down notes on the things I saw. The entries were made in little pocket notebooks, some brown, some black, some yellow. The spelling was erratic and the letters of the penciled words often headed in different directions. But the meaning of the sentences was clear.

"This morning," reads one entry, "I scratched my head in bed. The hairs rubed together and made a squeek. Tippie-Tail, the kitten, jumped on my head." Another notation records: "While I was walking acros an open space, a kingbird flue down and struck me. This kept up until I hollored. Then it quit. This afternoon, when I went acros the same place, it hapened again. I saw the bird had a nest in a near by tree." "Today," a third memorandum states, "I saw a baby chick on its mother's back and the mother was walking along, too." "I wandered in the woods today, making nature notes," says a fourth entry. "I picked a pocketfull of wintergreen berrys there and sat on a mossy log eating them while a song sparrow sang to me." "Under the big oak tree," I put down on another day, "when I was writing in this book, Tippie-Tail kept trying to rub his whiskers on the end of my pencil."

Some of the notations were short and factual, such as: "Hairs do not turn into snakes." "Mole's fir can turn anyway and will not hold mold." "When I was little, a friend and I found a bulfrog that wouldent fit into a quart pail." "Chips fly as far as nine paces from the tree when flickers are burrowing a hole."

In one of the notebooks, with a well-eroded pasteboard cover, I entered a census-list of all the creatures I had seen at Lone Oak. With the original spelling intact, it reads: "'Robin, night-halk, red-headed woodpeccar, bluebird, tad pole, high holor, swallow, tree toad, Virginia rale, rabit, morning dove, king fisher, mole, bat, cow, mink, meado mouse, song sparrow, eagle, buzard, dear mouse, coon, skunk, weasle, scarlit tanger, butcher bird, horse, blacksnake, gartersnake, rattelsnake, sheep, crain."

A whole notebook was labeled: "atmosphers." It was devoted to atmospheric bits and descriptive passages. Sample jottings follow: "In the top of the dead tree, two flickers noisily go up and down like see-saws." "The smoke is an aerial serpant." "Over Gunder's hill, the sunset was so red the rim of the hilltop looked like a prarie-fire was burning behind it." "Crybaby came to the door and mewed. She was covered with cobwebs." "Its too hot even to play. If there *is* a breeze, it seems afraid to move for fear it will get hot." "As the twylight lengthened, the only sounds were the 'Whack! Whack!' of an old man chopping wood and the 'Mooo!' of a brindel cow."

Most of my jottings were set down surreptitiously, out of the sight of people. William E. Barton, in his *The Life of Abraham Lincoln,* tells how he once encountered a small boy in a clearing among the mountains of Kentucky. He was standing beside a brook looking up at the sun coming over a range of hills and was repeating in a sing-song chant a rhyme that he had composed:

"Oh, Mountain, big and high:
I'll stand on you and I'll touch the sky!"

Each time he chanted it he listened to the echo of his voice. Suddenly he discovered the presence of a stranger on the little-traveled road. In embarrassment he slipped silently into the woods. Barton wanted to stop and talk to him, but the boy remained hidden. He was, as the author puts it, ashamed that he had been overheard in his dialogue with the high hill in whose shadow he dwelt.

Similarly, whenever strangers appeared on the road or called at the farm I hid my notebook and pencil. Because I was doing something different, something that nobody else I knew was doing, I had the feeling that I would be laughed at and considered queer. This deathly fear of ridicule remained with me for many years. It was only in later life that I learned the truth of the old adage: Sticks and stones they break my bones, but words they never hurt me! Words, in those early days, were sticks and stones that seemed to break my bones.

From earliest memory scenes around me impressed themselves deeply on my mind. Certain landscapes, together with the sounds, the smells, the activities of the moment, are still vivid after a lapse of decades. There is, in particular, one Lone Oak moment which has returned to me innumerable times.

A still winter day was drawing to its close. Gramp and

I had driven home from Michigan City with a bob-sled loaded with coal for the parlor stove. As we carried it into the cellar, a bushel-basketful at a time, our shoes squeaked on the hard-packed snow. The sunset, over Gunder's Hill, faded slowly into twilight in that perfect stillness which fills the air on certain nights of silent cold.

There was something in the wide hush of the mantled countryside, in the play of colors over the fields of snow; something in my physical condition of the moment, or in the sadness of an imminent return to school, or in the solemnity of the noiseless change from day to dark; something which impressed that sunset on my mind more than any other I have ever seen. I seemed transported into another world; I seemed dwelling on a timeless plain of color. Each time I issued from the deep dusk of the cellar the tinted snow and sky appeared more entrancing than before. In after years, on three or four occasions when winter day has been merging into windless dusk, I have felt remnants of that long-ago enchantment.

While the life of my wagonshed museum was relatively short—it ended with the return of the horse-drawn implements to their rightful places in the fall—the recording of observations in little notebooks continued for years thereafter. What the consequence was, and how this activity reached its natural climax, will be recorded on later pages of this book.

·22·

ATTIC HOURS

OVERHEAD the leaves of the great oak hung unmoving. Birds were silent. The cows lay in the shade chewing their cuds with closed eyes, and hens walked about with open beaks, croaking dismally. Only the small butterflies whirled and danced with unabated intensity. It was mid-afternoon and a great blanket of August heat had descended on the farm.

I lay on my back in a red-and-green hammock under the oak tree. Munching on an early harvest apple, I watched three sparrows dusting themselves listlessly in the roadway. Then I sat up. I had just remembered something.

All that summer I had forgotten to investigate the attic.

As a child I had a cat-like love of attics. There was always unexpected treasure to be discovered in the mysterious, dim light of the Lone Oak storeroom. It was a repository of history. Attic hours were entrancing journeys into the past.

When I reached the kitchen door Gram was putting carbolic acid and water on the screen to keep the flies away.

"Why on earth you have to pick the hottest day in all the year to go up in the attic is more than I can understand!" she commented.

"I didn't think of it before," I told her, as though that explained everything.

Climbing the narrow, white-painted stairs, I reached the upper floor. These stairs were hardly wider than Gramp's shoulders and they turned sharply at the top. The steps there were shaped like pieces of pie and you had to walk around the outer edge of the turn to find sufficient support for your feet. A yellowing Chinese straw-mat carpeted the low-ceilinged bedroom at the top of the stairs and an iron bed was pushed against the far wall. It supported a thick mattress and pillows stuffed with down from Gram's own poultry. It was into this bed that I tumbled nightly when Gram had ended the evening's reading and Gramp had cleared his throat and announced:

"Well, 'ts time fer honest folk t' be abed an' rogues a-joggin'."

At the point where the stairs reached the level of the

bedroom a painted wooden door, held shut with a wooden button, formed the entrance to the Lone Oak attic. When I swung the door back on its hinges a rush of hot air, as though from a blast furnace, struck me in the face. The interior, just under the peak of the dining-room roof where I had perched so often to view the distant dunes, had but a single source of ventilation. This was a small, round window at the far eastern end.

The attic was about sixteen feet long. But only the first half was covered with floorboards. I took especial delight in tightroping along the beams of the unfloored part. Between these beams there was nothing but the lath and plaster of the ceiling below. Gram was in continual fear that some day I would miss my footing and appear suddenly, falling through the wallpaper over the dining-room table.

At the door of the attic I took a deep breath and then crawled into the stifling interior. Half a dozen mud-daubers buzzed about in the still air. I could see their pale-yellow masonry cartridges attached to the timbers above my head. A large fly followed me through the open doorway, adding his higher-pitched buzzing to the drone of the wasps. I felt the rafters close above my head. They were hot to my touch. A few inches away the August sun was pouring its heat from a cloudless sky down onto the old shingles of the slanting roof. It now seems something of a miracle that, in this attic-oven, the piles of ancient magazines never caught fire from spontaneous combustion.

These piles of periodicals lay in shadowy heaps around me. The smell of old paper and dust was heavy in the air. Through a process of natural selection, the piles furthest back in the dim recesses of the attic were the most ancient, those near the door the most recent. It was among the former that I made the most interesting discoveries. There were *Ladies Home Journals* dating back long before the advent of Edward Bok. There were old copies of *Harper's Magazine, The Youth's Companion, McClure's Magazine, Everybody's,* and one periodical whose name I cannot remember which devoted whole pages to paintings of birds.

Somewhat like a wild duck, diving below the surface after food and returning to the air again, I grabbed magazines here and there and then bolted out of the door with my armload of dusty paper. Gram called from below:

"Edwin, if you don't keep out of that attic, you'll addle your brains!"

My head swam from the close heat. I lay on the floor with the retrieved magazines scattered around me on the straw-matting. Flies buzzed along the windowpanes and up and down the screens. Occasionally a faint breeze slipped through the window and ran along the floor and I would breathe deeply.

The story that held me fascinated that long, hot afternoon is one that I can recall vividly even today. It was in *The Youth's Companion* and it was written by C. A. Stephens, the author of a long series of tales about events on the Old Squire's farm, in Maine. Once, years later, I swung out of my way, on a trip through that state, to hunt up the site of the very farm where the Old Squire, Addison, Halstead, Theodora and the others had enjoyed the great years of their lives. The hero of those tales, I remember, eventually became a noted naturalist associated with Louis Agassiz.

In this particular story, which I had stumbled upon, the adventures revolved about a huge dog, Bender, a canine Dr. Jekyll and Mr. Hyde. By day he was a respected member of the community, by night the leader of an outlaw band of sheep-killing dogs. I recall how I trembled with anticipation as one of the boys hid in a sheepskin sack amid the flock to catch the mysterious night maurauders. And I recall how the dogs attacked the sack, mistaking it for a sleeping ewe, and how the boy leaped up from the doze into which he had fallen with a great cry of alarm which frightened off the outlaw animals. After that Bender was a roving Ishmael, with every man's hand against him. What befell him and his outlaw band, a footnote to the story announced, would be related in the following issue of the magazine.

I hurriedly compared the dates of magazines I had around me. The desired issue was not there. I plunged, in haste, back into the heat of the attic to emerge, panting, with another armload of *The Youth's Companion*. None of them was the one desired. Again and again I dove into the dim light and the stifling heat of the low room. Again and again I emerged with everything but the wanted magazine. I was wringing wet. When I appeared in the kitchen in search of a drink of cold water Gram cried:

"For Heaven's sake, child, where *have* you been?"

I looked at myself in the mirror. The dust had turned to streaks of mud on my perspiring face. I washed at the sink and climbed the stairs once more. Six additional armloads appeared from the attic door, and I was carting out miscellaneous magazines, before I pounced triumphantly upon the issue so diligently sought. Lying on my stomach amid the mounds of magazines, and oblivious to the future chore of replacing them all, I plunged happily into the rest of the story.

It was late in the afternoon when I finally reached the climax—the great dog and his band at bay within a mountain cavern; the farmers, who had cornered the outlaw animals, standing ready with rifles while flames leaped from stick to stick amid a high mound of wood which had been pushed into the entrance of the cave. And then that spine-tingling final moment when Bender, all hope gone, lifted his head within the smoke-filled cavern and gave voice to the long and mournful howl which was his death-song. It was all as real to me as the fly buzzing along the window-screen.

Another continued story which came from the attic had a less-satisfactory history.

Cowboys were battling bullet for bullet with cattle-rustlers in the first installment of an old *Argosy* adventure tale when Gram read: "To be continued." We never found the next issue and we never learned whether the hero, firing from under the belly of his leaping broncho, or the outlaw, blazing away from a clump of sagebrush, won the deadly duel. From the vantage-point of later experience with such works of fiction I think I can guess the answer. But then Gramp and I were on needles and pins with indecision.

Several mice which, along with the mud-daubers, inhabited the attic also contributed to my difficulties. These animals were my special enemies. I remember that once I stumbled upon a prize—a tale about trappers in the far Northwest—and then discovered that the mice had nibbled away the most exciting part in the runover columns. The nests of these rodents among the periodicals always seemed to be lined with pieces of the choicest adventure stories. Why they couldn't pick the fashion pages of *The Ladies Home Journal* was more than I could understand.

·23·

WE GO TO TOWN

GRAMP was poking me in the ribs and shouting: "Last call fer th' dinin' car!"

The bedroom windows were hazy gray rectangles facing the east. It was four o'clock in the morning and we were going to town.

A trip to town with Gramp was no ordinary journey. We were all astir by lamplight. The cracker-wagon had been stored with its load of potatoes and sweet corn and early apples the night before. While we rushed through the early chores, Gram got a hurried breakfast of fried mush and maple syrup. Then Gramp wheeled the horses into place and hooked the tugs. By four-thirty we were ready to go. As a final step Gramp and I changed into our "city clothes." This was a time of excitement and alarms.

"'Mimy," Gramp would call from the bedroom, "do y' suppose I've got a clean shirt somewhere hereabouts?"

"Of course you have!" Gram would answer indignantly. "You've always got a clean shirt in the middle drawer of the tall bureau. Just open the drawer and you'll see it."

I would hear Gramp mumble: "Here 't is. Ef it'd been a snake it'd a bit me!"

There would be a silence. Then I could hear him talking to himself. A moment later he would appear in the doorway with his necktie dangling from one hand.

"Mother," he would blurt out, "ef y' want me t' wear this blamed contraption, y'll have t' tie it fer me!"

Never so long as I knew him did he master the art of tying a four-in-hand. Once when he was on the Grand Jury, in Valparaiso, he went to bed every night from Monday to Friday with his shirt on.

"I was afraid t' unfasten that 'tarnal necktie," he explained. "I knew I'd never git it tied again."

To Gramp clothes were something to keep him warm in winter and to shelter him from the sun and rain in summer. If they accomplished this, they served the purpose of their existence and he asked no more. He refused ever to take more than one handkerchief.

"I haven't got a cold," he would say.

While Gram, intent on maintaining the reputation of the family, wimbled out my ears with the wet end of a washcloth and plastered down my thatch of unruly hair —which, she remarked in passing, looked "like the rats had slept in it"—Gramp would begin hunting for his hat. As long as I can remember, there was always an excited hunt for his best hat just at the moment of starting.

After the previous trip to town he had put it away specially in some place where it would be safe. Sometimes we would find it hanging on the corner of a picture-frame, sometimes back of the dining-room door, sometimes on top of the kitchen cupboard. If, by chance, someone had put it away on the closet-shelf, where it belonged, Gramp would say indignantly:

"No wonder I can't find my hat! It's hid away clear out o' sight!"

Finally all would be ready. We would climb up to the weathered wooden seat of the old cracker-wagon and Gramp would adjust a blanket over the baskets of fruit and potatoes to keep out the dust. Then with shouted "Good-byes"—as though we were departing for a long journey—we would rush down the lane and out into the sandy road that led to Michigan City.

That six-mile drive through the cool air of dawn was always filled with beauty and interest. Birds were awakening, rabbits were out in the open fields, and in the lowland hollows sheets of luminous mist glowed in the sunrise. This was the hour that the French painter, Corot, strove throughout his life to portray on canvas. "The sun is risen," he used to say. "All things break forth—glistening, glittering and shining in a full flood of light. It is adorable.

I paint! I paint! A little later, the sun, aflame, burns the earth. Everything becomes heavy. *We can see too much now.* Let us go home."

Usually Gramp and I took produce to market about once a week, but at times when sweet corn or string beans were in season we sometimes went to Michigan City every other day for a week or so. One morning, during such a period, we passed a neighbor's field where he was doing some early hoeing before the heat of the day.

"Ed," he called, "what y' goin' t' town so soon again fer?"

"Th' clock's stopped," Gramp replied with a wink at me. "We hev t' go t' town t' see what time 't is!"

True to his pioneer spirit, Gramp soon tired of the tameness of traveling the same route to the city. For a time he would take the old Chicago road, coming into the city past the gray walls of the state penitentiary. Then he would switch and go by way of the Carver schoolhouse. Sometimes we would come into town along Tenth Street, past Billy Miller's meat market; at other times we would approach from the south, rolling over the red brick pavement of Ohio Street. One summer Gramp insisted on going out of his way on each trip to the city in order to stop at a "health spring" that bubbled out of a clay bank. The water had a sulphurous, repulsive odor. But Gramp insisted we drink long draughts for our stomachs' sake.

As we rode along he sometimes told me about Michigan City as it was in 1854, when he first saw it as a boy of thirteen. Then it was a dreary settlement of about 1,500 inhabitants. To keep wagon-wheels from sinking in the sand, planks had been laid along the main street. It was known as The Grand Plank Road. The only bank in town, a bank whose money was good only in the county, was known as the Plank Road Bank and the money was called Grand Plank money. Soon after they had come west Gramp and one of his brothers picked two milkpails full of wild dewberries and carried them six miles to the city to trade for a piece of pork.

"We had tough sleddin' in those days," he said. "Many a time we didn't hev meat enough t' grease th' pan."

By the time our cracker-wagon reached the city limits, women were up and we proceeded to skim the cream of customers before the stores opened. We would drive down a street and Gramp would yell:

"Apples! Potatoes! Sweet corn!"

When customers appeared from the houses, I would jump down and measure out the desired peck of potatoes or half bushel of apples. An annual agreement was that if I picked up the good apples for Gramp, I could sell the small and wormy ones at reduced prices for myself. To Gramp's disgust, my inferior, half-priced apples usually sold out first of all. On some days nobody seemed to want to buy anything.

"Mebby there's been a run on th' bank!" Gramp would say.

After we had plodded up and down half a dozen side-streets, on one such day, without selling a single potato or apple, Gramp got desperate. He decided to add a new flourish to his call. He shouted:

"Apples! Potatoes! Sweet corn! *Bananas!*"

Two women appeared immediately. Both asked for bananas. Gramp's ears got red. He mumbled something about the bananas not being fully ripe yet and we drove hastily around the corner.

Before noon our load of produce usually had been changed into cash. With money jingling in my pocket, I would turn to the pleasures of the day. Leaving Deck and Colty hitched to the iron pipe at Sixth and Main Streets, we would, first of all, head for the Canditorium.

During the preceding days, when I had been digging potatoes—with the smell of hot dry dust in my nostrils and the weight of the burning sunshine on my back—I had dreamed of this moment: of opening the screen door, of entering the cool, dim interior, of pulling back a chair with the faint, complaining screech of metal on tile, of looking over the printed menu, of weighing all the virtues of all the concoctions, of always deciding on the same thing—a wintergreen soda—and of that final blissful moment when—with its pink foam rising like sunset-tinted clouds—the soda was set before me. All now became an actuality.

Gramp and I always ceremoniously treated each other to sodas. At first we compromised on who should pay for the treat. I paid for his soda and he paid for mine. Then I hit upon a better plan. It brought satisfaction to all, even to the proprietor of the store. I treated Gramp, paying for his soda as well as my own, and then he treated me in a turnabout procedure. In this way we had two wintergreen sodas without feeling we had been unduly extravagant.

It always took our eyes a minute or two to accustom themselves to the dim lighting of the Canditorium when we came in from the glaring sunshine outside. Once, when I looked around as my eyes became accustomed to the semi-dusk, I noticed a lady sitting with several companions at a corner table. She was wearing one of the less fortunate creations of the milliner's art—a barrel-like hat with a single bedraggled feather rising upright from the top. I nudged Gramp:

"Isn't that a funny hat, Gramp?" I whispered.

"What'd y' say?"

"I said, isn't that a funny hat that woman's got on?"

"What woman? What hat? I can't hear y' unless y' speak up."

I said: "Never mind."

Just then he caught sight of the hat himself.

"Thet *is* a funny hat," he said in a stage whisper. "Looks like she's got on a churn."

Our thirst quenched for the time-being by the two wintergreen sodas, we began shopping. While Gramp bought the groceries, I stocked up on Jumbo wintergreen gum, got some peppermint candies for Gram, and prowled among the magazines at the bookstore. Our final stop was the real high point of the day. This was the Michigan City Public Library, cool under its great elms and with the lawns around it freshly sprinkled.

I knew the interior of this square graystone building almost as well as I did the fields of Lone Oak. With a pile of returning books under my arm, I would enter the quiet building filled with the mingled, mysterious smell of old leather, stored books, and piles of magazines and papers. On one wall there was a case containing thirty-three mounted butterflies, the first that I had ever seen, and I used to stand fascinated by their shapes and colors. The librarians there were always kind to us and few buildings in the world have meant more to me than this gray storehouse of learning and adventure.

With another armload of books—animal stories, natural histories, adventure novels, volumes on aviation—I would reappear after the lapse of half an hour or so and we would set out for home.

There was one more event which crowned the pleasures of the day. On our leisurely progress out of town we used to stop at Glidden's Bakery for fresh buns. A little farther on we halted at Billy Miller's butcher shop for a six-inch piece of bologna. At the grocery store next door we bought a large bottle of Lomax root beer. Restraining ourselves as best we could, we waited until we had reached the turn by Doran's woods before we pulled up in the shade to dine at leisure.

With Gramp's jackknife we would cut open the buns and slice off pieces of bologna to make sandwiches. Then we would knock the cap off the root beer bottle on the hub of a front wheel and imbibe foaming draughts that held the flavor of roots and herbs, of sassafras and wintergreen.

After that we rode on in silence, the traces creaking, the hoofs of the horses clumping steadily in the soft sand, the grasshoppers shrilling from the fields and the cicadas from the trees overhead. I usually became lost in one of the books, suddenly waking up to reality as we passed O'Keefe's woods and came in sight of Lone Oak.

It was usually mid-afternoon, or at sunset, when we reached home. That night we would hurry through the chores, feeding the chickens and pigs and cows and horses, collecting the eggs and bringing in the wood for the kitchen stove. When Gramp had milked and Gram had the supper dishes washed and put away, we would settle down with eager anticipation. Gram would adjust her silver-rimmed spectacles, turn up the lamp-wick, and begin the first of the story-books—books that we had never heard of before, books usually by authors whose names were unknown to us, books that had been resting, like machines thrown out of gear, on the shelves of a library but a few short hours before.

·24·

LAMPLIGHT

A FAMOUS explorer once told me that he never started on an expedition without packing *Alice in Wonderland* in his luggage. He had read it a hundred times or more—in the light of jungle campfires, amid the crags and plateaus of remote mountains, beneath cabin lamps on ships moored in lonely bays. The adventures of Alice and the Gryphon, the Mad Hatter and the March Hare, the Cheshire Cat and the Queen of Hearts, had thus been linked, in retrospect, with strange peoples and bizarre surroundings. In his mind the pages of this childhood classic could evoke images of coral reefs and rain forests, of outlandish coasts and storms at sea.

So, for all of us, the books that have affected us deeply and the surroundings where they have been read are linked in memory. The poems of Swinburne, for me, always bring to mind a wide, placid river flowing slowly, irresistibly through a country of drooping willows and high, eroded banks. The haze of twilight lies over the empty water. My rowboat turns languidly around and around as it drifts downstream. It was thus, during an adventurous summer of my college years when I rowed four hundred miles down the Ohio River to the Mississippi, that I first encountered the rich imagery and the sonorous lines of Swinburne.

King Lear, his wild white hair and beard flying in the great storm on the heath, is similarly linked in memory with the waiting room of a dingy inter-urban station at Morris, Ill. There I first read the play from end to end one sultry Sunday afternoon when I had missed connections and was marooned for hours. For me the wit and valor of Rostand's Cyrano de Bergerac is joined in memory with the image of a lonely river-bank west of Wichita, in Kansas; Henri Amiel's *Journals* with a green park bench amid the skyscrapers of Manhattan; the thoughts of Marcus Aurelius with the sycamores of a meandering creek in Indiana; and Boswell's *Life of Johnson* with a straggling grove of eucalyptus trees on a headland of the California coast.

But more vividly than any of these associations, the images of Lone Oak surroundings are joined with books.

Merely the titles of some of those entrancing early volumes —*When Wilderness Was King, The Green Mountain Boys, The Deerslayer, Barriers Burned Away, Wings of the Morning*—are sufficient to bring back the crying of the whippoorwills, the smell of the kerosene lamp, the fluttering of moth-wings along the lighted window-screens, as Gram read on and on during those long-ago summer nights.

Heinrich Heine, the poet, tells in his autobiography—a little wistfully—of the undying impression made upon him by his first book of fiction. His parents intended him for a career in business and purposely kept him ignorant of the whole world of imaginative literature. Thus it happened that when he encountered his first volume of fiction —*The Life and Adventures of the Ingenious Gentleman Don Quixote de la Mancha,* by Miguel de Cervantes—he accepted it as a book of fact.

"I was still a very small boy," he relates. "I stole from the house in the early morning and hurried away to the Palace gardens, there to read Don Quixote in peace. Spring, in bloom, lay listening in the still morning light and had her praises sung by the nightingale, her sweet flatterer. I sat upon a mossy old bench of stone in the Avenue of Sighs, as they call it, not far from the waterfall and charmed my little heart with the brave adventures of the bold knight. I took it all in earnest and however laughably the poor hero might be the sport of Fate, I thought it must be so.

"Dulcinea's knight rose higher and higher in my esteem

and won ever more my love the longer I read the wonderful book, and this I did every day in the garden, so that by autumn I had come to an end of the history—and never shall I forget the day when I read of the sorrowful encounter in which the knight was so shamefully laid low!

"It was a sad day. Ugly clouds scudded across the gray sky, the yellow leaves fell down drearily from the trees, heavy tear drops hung upon the last flowers; the song of the nightingale had died away; on all sides I was forced to see the signs of mortality, and my heart was like to break when I read how the noble knight, crushed and confounded, lay upon the ground and without raising his visor, as though he spoke from the grave, in a sick weak voice said to the victor: 'Dulcinea is the most beautiful lady in the world and I am the most unfortunate knight upon the earth, but it is not seemly that my weakness should blaspheme this truth—therefore, knight, make an end with thy lance!' Alas! This famous Knight of the Silver Moon, who overcame the bravest and noblest man in the world, was a barber in disguise!"

Although we knew, at Lone Oak, the difference between books of fact and books of fiction, we lost ourselves completely in the more exciting tales. The purring sound of Gramp's pipe would increase its tempo and I would lie, round-eyed, on the dining-room floor while the stories unfolded themselves, chapter by chapter. Some of the books which made the deepest impression on me at the time were *Eben Holden,* by Irving Bacheller; *The Crisis* and *The Crossing,* by Winston Churchill; *The Sky Pilot,* by Ralph Connor; *The Riverman*, by Stewart Edward White; *The Wolf Hunters*, by James Oliver Curwood; and the novels of Cooper, Dickens, and Mark Twain. All were exciting tales and most of them concerned the out-of-doors.

One summer we found a book of non-fiction that was as thrilling as the most exciting novel. It was a thick volume of more than 600 pages and we had to renew it at the library several times before we came to the final page. It was Paul du Chaillu's story of his explorations in darkest Africa. In vivid detail it told of his encounters with crocodiles, bull elephants, rhinoceroses, jungle serpents, and huge gorillas. As the story went on and on, Gram used to get out *Montieth's Geography* and we would follow, down the rivers and into the jungle areas, the progress of our hero.

Another non-fiction book, a thin volume with green covers and woodcut illustrations of volcanoes and cannibals in outrigger canoes, also sent me to the geography, seeking maps relating to the other side of the globe from Africa. This volume told of adventures in the South Sea Islands. It had been published by a missionary society and had found its way to the bookshelves which had been built along one wall in the parlor at Lone Oak.

The juvenile books which we read at that time began with Kingsley's *The Water Babies* and ran through a range which included *The Four Boy Hunters, Adventures of a Brownie, Helen's Babies,* and *The Motor Boys.* One juvenile book, first read when I was about eight, had a powerful effect upon me—an effect which continued for years thereafter. This was *The Real Diary of a Real Boy,* by Henry A. Shute.

Shute was a New Hampshire lawyer and judge who wrote books of humor in his spare time. His best-selling story of the doings of "Plupy Shute" was written in the misspelled vernacular popular among humorists of the time. I bought a composition book in Michigan City and began recording the events of the day at Lone Oak. Unfortunately, Plupy Shute was my model and my master.

I sought to add humor by orthographic eccentricities. This training, added to a natural inclination for ignoring the dictates of Webster, ruined whatever spelling ability I may have possessed. Throughout grade-school and in high school and college, and even when I had a graduate degree from an eastern university, my spelling was a stumbling-block and a by-word. The longer, more difficult words—which I had learned in later life—I could spell correctly while the commonplace, simple words, that everybody knew, were the ones I was most likely to misspell. Thus my deficiency was obvious to all.

Years later, when I was earning my living as an editorial writer, a friendly editor reached the end of his patience.

"Who is this B-a-c-c-u-s you mention?" he asked.

"That's the Greek god."

"Well, his name is spelled B-A-C-C-H-U-S. B-a-c-c-u-s doesn't spell anything—except ignorance!"

Decades passed, and I had begun to make Webster's Dictionary my constant writing companion, before the effects of Plupy Shute began gradually to dissipate. At Lone Oak the large dictionary on its upright stand was considered by me as merely a repository for interesting pictures of airplanes and birds and butterflies. I used to spend hours, standing first on one foot and then on the other, poring over these familiar picture-pages. Other memorable picture-mines at Lone Oak were *Wood's Natural History* and *Steele's Popular Zoology.*

Nature books of various kinds formed an important item on our literary bill-of-fare. Gram had definite preferences in her likes and dislikes among books of the kind. One evening, when "the weary and unintelligible weight of the world," and the ways of mankind, were too much for her, she said:

"I don't like stories that make animals talk and act like humans. The reason I *like* animals is because they *aren't* like humans!"

Among the favorites which I begged Gram to read again and again were *Shaggycoat,* the story of a beaver, by Clarence Hawkes; *Red Fox,* by Charles G. D. Roberts; and *Bears of Blue River,* by Charles Major. Above them all were those classics of their kind, the early animal stories of Ernest Thompson Seton. I have no idea how many times we read *Wild Animals I Have Known, The Trail of the Sandhill Stag, Two Little Savages, The Biography of a Grizzly,* or *Lives of the Hunted.*

But I remember that oftenest of all we turned to that thrilling story of *Krag, the Kootenay Ram*—reading again and again the tale of Scotty MacDougall's long pursuit, of the death of the great mountain sheep, and of the climax in which the avalanche avenged his killing. Although I knew the story by heart, I always gripped my chair and felt a tingle running down my spine when Gram came to those final sentences:

"All that day, the White Wind blew. . . . It sang a wild, triumphant battle-song, and the strain of the song was:

> I am the mothering White Wind;
> This is my hour of might.
> The hills and the snows are my children;
> My service they do tonight.

"And here and there, at the word received, there were mighty doings among the peaks. . . . Down the Gunder peak there whirled a monstrous mass charged with a mission of revenge. Down, down, down, loud *snoofing* as it went, and sliding on from shoulder, ledge, and long incline, now wiping out a forest that would bar its path, then crashing, leaping, rolling, smashing over cliff and steep descent, still gaining as it sped. Down, down, faster, fiercer, in one fell and fearful rush, and Scotty's shanty, and all that it contained, was crushed and swiftly blotted out. The Ram's own Mother White Wind, from the western sea, had come—had long delayed, but still had come at last."

In a way, during the evenings of those golden summer days, my passionate love of the out-of-doors and my interest in the world of books found a common meeting-ground. I even dreamed of some glorious, far-off future—shrouded in a sort of glowing mist—when I, too, would write a book. I began to jot down expanded notes about the activity of the wild creatures around me and all the moods of Nature. I plunged into writing with all the intensity of a new enthusiasm.

That enthusiasm has burned on after so much that then surrounded it has passed away. A curious enchantment, with its lonely battles and its peculiar satisfactions, it remained the constant star through the long later years, the years of tacking and zigzagging, of making the best of other work, of indecision and despair.

·25·

WHITE TIP

THE wild birds, the small animals, and especially the cats, at Lone Oak were the subjects of some of my earliest attempts at writing.

A numerous population of cats and kittens—black-and-white, calico, and tabby—lived about the barn. At milking time they would rub, purring, against Gramp's legs. Occasionally he would relieve the monotony of his task by directing a thin, white stream of milk into the open mouth of a mewing kitten. It would blink its eyes tight shut and splutter in surprise. Then its eyes would pop open, its pink tongue would appear—running along its whiskers—and it would begin to lick itself with purring satisfaction. Often times I lined up, open-mouthed, along with the kittens.

Every cat at Lone Oak had its own name. Gram tended to that. Some summers the increase in cat population taxed her ingenuity. The pets which I remember most vividly were Old Kitty Flannigan, Tippie-Tail, Snip-in-Diaz, Little Snip, Crybaby, Rose-of-the-Army, and Old Black Joe.

Sitting on a three-legged milking stool, or dangling my legs over one of the great rough-hewn beams of the hay-loft, or leaning back against the ridged bark of the lone oak, I used to set down, in hurried scrawls, the doings of the cats.

"His eyes blazed," reports one of these entries concerning a big fight beside the barn door. "His mussels tightened and he sprang foreward and chalenged the stranger to prove his worthyship."

"One day," says another notation, "Crybaby was prowling about the woodpile. She aspyed a rabit hopping leasurlearly about nipping off tender blades of gras. She flattened out like a linx and cralled toards her quarrery whos back was turned. As she sprang, her claws came out like rows of needels. Crybaby landed square on the rabits back and gave it no chanch to cry out. With one nip and sweep, its life was cut short. Crybaby picked up the limp body, as if it were a kitten, and troted off under the barn."

One of the barnyard kittens, Little Snip, was even celebrated in verse which I set down on a piece of scratch paper one June day when I was seven. The lines ran:

"Once I had a kitty
And she was aughful pritty.
She had the pinkest little nose
And the finest padded toes.
She was a reglar rover
And wandered the country over."

During the winter when I was eight, and was attending the Woodlawn School in Joliet, one of the teachers asked us to write out an imaginary story in class. After chewing my pen-holder for a while, I launched into "My Life Among the Mountains." It began:

"When I was young I lived in Missouri but when I became older I went to seek my forten in the western country of Montana. Here I expected to buy a clame and mine. But ill-forten had befallen me and now I was a wanderer in the mountains.

"One day, I was climbing up a steap gulley when I noticed a grait smoke raising in the air. 'O, it's—' and then I slipped into a grait, hurling, mad torent of water.'—a forest fire!' I thought. Coyots, deer, bare and other animals plunged into the water and I saw their skinn was singed. Hundreds and hundreds of wild animals came snorting, plunging, and ducking into the water up to their nostrals. There was a shower of sparkes and a grait leap of flaim and then a roar that was deafning. Hundreds and hundreds of animals were killed out right and many were mortaly woonded.

"The fire was extinguished when it reached the mountain stream. I built a log hut and was buissy fore three weeks in skining and preparing the meat and skins. I had three thousand firs, 1 thousand hides, and so mutch meat that I waisted more than six tons of meat and buzards and hakks came in millions."

At that point, while I was lost in fantasy, the class came to an end. I asked if I could finish up the story at home. Thereafter, for a week or more, I wrote on and on. Each noon I used to run all the way home, over the half-mile or so of limestone sidewalks, to gobble down my lunch and then plunge into "My Life Among the Mountains." Day after day I went back to the teacher for more paper. As the story unfolded the adventures became wilder and wilder. Without wasted words I jumped from one spine-tingling situation to another. I had just escaped from a whirlpool, for example, when:

" 'I see the mill!' I shouted glefully and ran at all posibal speed. 'Well!' I gasped and stoped stock still fore I saw two men set fuses to grait cans of nightragrissaleen and then run away. I leaped to the fuses and splashed water on them. Then I grabed both rascals by the colar and marched them up to a shed and locked them in the swine-pen. After a long time on a diet of bred and water, they confessed that they were the fellos ho blew up the mines."

By the time I was ready to hand in the completed story a good-sized bundle of pages had been covered, front and back, with my somewhat illegible script. The teacher, who had been waiting with considerable curiosity for the product of my labors, received the bundle with expressions of amazement and encouragement.

Other literary projects of various kinds followed in rapid order. For several months I was engrossed in getting out a one-sheet publication, with no circulation at all, called *The Naturelist's Weekly*. It contained short items on the doings of wild creatures and the events of the season out-of-doors. *Dan's Diary*, the imaginary record of a trapper in the wild west, kept me out of mischief for weeks on end.

But the main current of my effort ran in the direction of Seton-type animal stories. There were: *Hop, the Toad; Bright-Eyes, the Great Horned Owl; Kadunka, the Bullfrog King of the Pond; Yellow-Back, the Cougar of Puget Sound; The Call of the Sunrise* (the biography of a woodchuck), and *The Call of the Twilight* (the biography of a raccoon). *Ranger, the Tale of a Snipe* ran on for half a hundred pages and *Roving Spot, the Cat that Went Wild* was even longer.

The latter story told of the life and times of a black-and-white kitten that became lost and went wild in the sand-dunes. It became the leader of a whole band of outlaw cats that prowled about the countryside after nightfall like a band of wolves. The tale ended in a smashing climax. A great forest fire, sweeping across the dunes, killed most of the band of marauders. Spot, escaping to a clearing around some farm buildings, became reunited with the boy from whom he had become separated years before.

Another story of that time, one of the few which did not concern the dunes or Lone Oak Farm, was entitled *The Engine Cat.* It was based on the life of a pet in the Michigan Central roundhouse at Joliet. The animal was a special favorite of the workmen, who fed it bits of meat from their dinner-pails. It took a particular fancy to one of the engineers and used to follow him into the cab of his locomotive, curling up in a corner of his seat near the boiler of the engine. In this position it would ride 150 miles on the round-trip to Michigan City. The animal was finally killed in an accident. It was run over by the engine, which was being backed into the roundhouse. At the throttle of the locomotive was the animal's special friend, the engineer. I remember that I sobbed bitterly when I came to this tragic climax of my story.

But it was neither *Roving Spot* nor *The Engine Cat* which I considered my masterpiece at the time. This was the story of a bald eagle, called *White Tip, the King of the Dunes.* From my lookout, on the rooftop at Lone Oak, I used to lie for a long time after the passing of an eagle overhead, wondering about its life and its adventures above the lake and the hills of sand. Out of this wondering grew the story of White Tip; Iron Claw, its father; and of "Cubby" Martin, the solitary hunter who pursued the bird as Sandy MacDougall had followed the Kootenay Ram.

During much of one summer I wrote and rewrote the pages, chewing the end of my pencil, scratching out and erasing, reading the story aloud to myself behind the granary and the barn. The tale began:

"The sun of a misty morning in June was piercing the dence drapries and glistning on the seemingly limmitless waist of sand with its mounds and barren tops. Upon one of these high dunes that looked out over the deep blue misty lake with its rolling white-capped waves and its ships, just descernable in the faint light, there stood a large pine leaning out over the edge. It was not a bushy pine by any means but in the middle there were a fiew scrub limbs and above them towered the massive bauld head of Iron Claw."

From that beginning the story followed through the nest-life of White Tip, the eaglet; its early adventures in the air; its long flight South and its return the following spring; its supremacy as the aerial king of the dune-country; and, finally, its death at the hands of Cubby Martin. This climax came when a great stranger eagle appeared above the dunes and challenged White Tip:

"As the stranger flew toards his pine, White Tip gave a screem. At the crie, the stranger stoped and poised in the air, his eyes fixed intently upon the Monark. The bark of the limb whair White Tip was purched fell rattling to the ground, clawed off by the nurvous, restless moving of his tallons.

"Suddenly, the stranger darted strait for the limb. White Tip sat still untill the bird was nearly upon him. Then he droped under and lay motionless, hiden from view.

"I was not the only observer of this battle of the air.

Cubby Martin had seen it, two. He sat on a bench at the door of his cabin, his repeter across his knees, watching White Tip with intrest. When he droped under the limb, the stranger came cloce. White Tip attacked from the bottom. Opening his beak, he drove it with inchredable speed into the side of his opoinant, at the same time diging in with his dedly tallons. They struggled for life or death, writhing and snapping, with beady eyes lit with firey hatred of each other.

"A sneeky sperit came into Cubby's mind. 'Now's my chanch!' he said and putting down his conchience, he ran toards the dune. His conchience kept whispering to him but he heeded it not. The birds tussled and fought with aufull malace; they came cloce to the earth; they bit and clawed like tigers. Cubby came creeping cloce. He hesitated a moment and then lifted his rifle and shot twice in rapid succusion. When he looked up, they both were quiet. An aufull stillness had settled down. Even the birds stoped churping. It seemed to Cubby as if he couldent stand it.

"Afterwards, he got the twenty-five dollars he had been promissed for White Tip. But he would have given twice that to have him alive once more. The storms beat upon the pine, year after year, and at last it rotted away and only a gray-haired old man was left to tell of the happy days when White Tip and Iron Claw ruled among the dunes."

Gramp and Gram were greatly impressed by this eagle story. I remember one painful Sunday afternoon when they insisted, aided and abetted by my mother, that the author appear in person and read the story aloud before visiting company.

They corralled me, washed my face, slicked down my hair, put me in a white shirt with a sailor-collar, and led me—as Gramp said later—"sidling along like a hog going to war" into the parlor. At last it was all over. I was turned free and I whisked into my normal clothes and disappeared until the dust of the departing carriages settled over the driveway.

·26·

TALES OF LONE OAK

HOWEVER, my perspiring personal appearance on that Sunday afternoon bore important fruit. The visitors, with that light-heartedness which characterizes those who have no financial obligations in the matter, were unanimous in the opinion that I should have a typewriter in order to submit my stories in presentable form to the publishers.

I echoed the idea in the days that followed. Gramp and Gram agreed. My mother added her endorsement. We all looked at my father. He would have to foot the bill. He was also, he hastened to say, in favor of the idea. But he didn't see how he could afford to buy a typewriter just then.

When I returned home, in September, I began filling in each lull in conversation at the dinner-table with sales-talks on the vital importance of owning a typewriter. I showed my father advertisements in newspapers and magazines. I priced the various models in the stores in Joliet. There I met my stumbling-block. The model I was most interested in cost an enormous sum—more than a hundred dollars. So, for a long time, the typewriter hung like an impossible goal before my eyes.

One night in November my father came home from work with a railroadman's magazine rolled up in his empty dinner-pail. He washed himself and sat down at the kitchen table. After he had put pork-chop gravy on his mashed potatoes and had taken the edge off his appetite, he stopped with his fork in mid-air. As though he had just thought of something, he remarked:

"Edwin, maybe we can get you a typewriter, after all."

My mother looked surprised. This was news to her. Like a hungry bumblebee attacking a clump of clover, I plied my father with a sudden buzz of questions. He remained mysterious until supper was over. Then he opened his dinner-pail and pulled out the rolled-up magazine.

"There is an advertisement in here," he said, "for a typewriter almost exactly like the one you want. I can get it for fifty-nine dollars."

My mother and I both reached for the magazine. A little hesitantly, my father handed it over. Across the top of one of the pulpwood advertising pages, printed in block type and capital letters, ran the sentence:

"360 CIGARS AND ONE REBUILT UNDERWOOD TYPEWRITER FOR ONLY $59."

My mother laughed. Then she compressed her lips and gave my father a severe look. He coughed apologetically. Shortly thereafter I was sent off to bed to get "a good long night's rest." I heard my parents talking at length in the kitchen. The next morning my father announced a little triumphantly that I was going to get my typewriter.

It came, after a lapse of several weeks, together with a box of cigars that looked like a small trunk. The typewriter was installed on a solid wooden table in an upper room. It seemed as heavy as a cart, as big as a desk, and as noisy as a threshing-machine. The initial, and most noticeable, effect of my possessing a typewriter was an increase in the general confusion caused by my erratic spelling through the insertion of a generous sprinkling of strange new marks—such as %, ¶, $, &, #, and *—among the words of my manuscripts.

In the optimistic rush of enthusiasm during my sales-talks to my father, I had gaily predicted that, if I owned a typewriter, I could sell enough stories within a few weeks to cover the cost of the machine. As a sad matter of record, fifteen years went by before my income from writing totaled the half-a-hundred and nine dollars the typewriter had cost.

At the time the machine arrived I was engaged in finishing up the *magnum opus* of the period. This was a book of twenty-five chapters entitled "Tales of Lone Oak." It was begun in June, 1908, a few weeks after I was nine years old, and was completed in December, 1909, when I was ten.

The starting of the book remains a vivid recollection. Gram was ironing in the kitchen. The house was redolent with the rich smell of beeswax which she occasionally applied to her heated iron. I was hunched over the dining-room table scribbling with a pencil on a pad of lined writing-paper. At the top of the first page I had placed the words: "TAILS OF LONE OAK," and, under it, the magic notation: "Chapter I."

By the time Gramp came up from the lower cornfield for his mid-morning snack of crackers and cheese and a drink of water, I had filled the first page with the opening scene of the book. Gram had me read it to Gramp. I have before me now the page, spelling and all, as I then saw it:

"Chapter I
Under The Walnut Tree

"It was a warm, or fairley hot, day in spring. The gras was turning green and the buding trees sent a plesant odor thru the evning air. The patient lowing of the cattle in the lain was distinctley heard above the skufling on the roosts of the chicken-coop and the grunting and squeeling from the pig-pen and the blating of the hungry calves. Sparrows churped loudly from the tamerak in frunt of the house and from the woods across the road came the song of the whip-por-will."

From that beginning I advanced—in spurts and stops —page after page and chapter after chapter. The adventures I had with Verne Bradfield, in and around Lone Oak, during the two summers when he lived near by, formed the theme of the book. The latter part of the first chapter told of our initial meeting on the day after the evening described above:

"I sat on the drag in the field acros the road, by the woods. Maine Fuller, ower hired man, was resting the team. A large walnut tree grew beside a big red barn on the next farm. Under it stood a boy of about seven years of age. He had a big straw-hat on his head and wore overalls with one suspender. His eyes were gray, turning dark and sometimes light. When angrey or exsited, his eyes would turn light and dark in rapid succession. His bare feet were sun-burned and his skin was hard so the rough clods did not hurt his feet.

"Just then he set down the cat he was playing with and looked toards us. After a fiew minutes of staring on both sides, Maine, who knew him well, called out:

" 'Say, Verne, here's a little boy about your size. Come on, you can play together and have a good time.'

" 'You can go over and play,' he announced to me.

"I timidly walked to the fence and stood. Verne sized me up and said impaishantly:

" 'Come on, have some fun!'

"I ammeaditly craled threw the fence and said bashfully:

" 'Have you got a very big hay-loft?'

" 'O, not so very big. But a pritty good-sized one. Come on and look at it.'

"I followed him threw the barn and up a ladder to the loft. Mr. Bradfield, Verne's father, was a carpinter and painter by trade but out in the country he got little to do. He now had a little farm of nine akers. His chief profit came from early and lait straw-berrys and very early peaches.

"The roomy loft was half full of hay and cornstalks. A big two-by-four was across the middle and to this we climed and cralled out slowley tell we reached the middle under which lay a pile of hay. Verne stood up and jumped to the pile below. I tried to follow his example but as I was about to arise, I fell head first and gave my neck sutch a rench that I dident try it again in a hurry. Verne laughted and laughted tell I began to too, to see him so tickled.

"I don't know when we would of stoped if a call hadent interupted our lafter:

" 'Edwin! Edwin!'

"I ran for the ladder but Verne was two quick. He was on the ladder and climing down before I had reached it. As I dismounted slowly and werrley, he lafed and pulled my foot. I clung tight and my feet dangled in the air. At this sight, Verne burst out into a roar of lafter and showed me how to regain the step again. I ran from the barn with Verne at my heels. I climed over the gait and ran toards the house.

" 'Got to stay in?' he called after me.

" 'I don't know. But I think not,' I replied on the run.

" 'If you don't be sure and come back!' he ejaculated.

" 'Yes,' was my ansure.

"I reached the house and asked Gram what she wanted.

" 'O, I only wanted to know whair you were,' she ansured as she turned to enter the house.

" 'I was over playing with Verne Bradfield. Can I go again?' I inquired.

" 'Yes, but not very long, thoe,' she replied as she shut the door.

"I went back on a dog-trot.

" 'U-h-o-o-o- Ver-ne!' I called.

" 'Come on!' came from somewhair.

"I looked around and caut Verne's head bobing in the corncrib. I climed over the gait to the corncrib and threw open the door but thair was know sight of Verne. In fear he would drop down on me, I ran to an open piece whair he could not approach without my knolage. A laugh came from the corncrib and I saw him dismounting on the logs from above the door.

" 'You couldent find me!' he burst out.

"I went up and looked in the corncrib. Then I went in and Verne followed me. We both climed up and sat on a log.

" 'Come on, this isent any fun!" ejaculated Verne and climed down. I followed and we looked at the chickens.

" 'Come out in the road and play!' I ejaculated, starting toards the fence.

" 'I can't. I gotto stay in the yard all day.'

" 'O, what will we do?' I inquired, coming back.

" 'Say Edwin, help me with my work, will you?' he inquired.

" 'Allright, what you got to do?'

" 'O, just shut up the chickens and a fiew things,' he ansured as he turned toards the chicken coop. I followed and helped chase, capture and settle the hens.

" 'Come on and feed Sam now,' he announced.

" 'Who is Sam?' I inquired in fear it was a pursin.

" 'O, ower horse, old Sam,' he replyed as he picked up a bushel basket and started toards the barn. I followed him.

" 'O, I thought it was somebody!'

"At this, he gave a harty laugh. Sam paishantly neighed.

" 'Here Sam,' called Verne cherrly as he pitched a fork full of hay into the mainger.

" 'You're a nice old Horse, aint you Sam?' he said stroaking Sam's nose and neck.

" 'Say, I think you're a nice boy,' he said, coming closer. 'I'm glad we met!' he added.

" 'So am I!' I agreed.

" 'We'll just play all the time,' ansured Verne. 'I'll show you all this country if you stay all summer.'

" 'I'll have to go home pritty soon,' I said. 'Gram said I couldent stay very long.'

" 'You got a gun?' Verne asked.

" 'Know, have you?'

" 'Know. But I want one!' he excleamed.

" 'O, I've gotto go, good-buy!' I called out.

" 'Come back in the morning!' he called after me.

" 'Sure I will!' was my ansuring call as I ran toards the house.

" 'This has been a happy day,' I said to Grandma as she tucked me in my little bed."

Thus ended Chapter I.

The other chapters—carrying such varied headings as: The First Quarrel, Water and Doit, An Exighting Hunt, A Trip After Cows, By the Ditch-Side, Inocent Theift, Doves in the Hayloft, Kittens in the Mainger, Woodcraft, Threw the Fence, and A Trip to the Grist-Mill—were written over a period of eighteen months. The pages of the scratchpads, on which the words were put down in pencil, were gathered together as each chapter was completed and put away in a pasteboard box. The chapters were held together by means of common pins or safety pins or hairpins, which were thrust through the paper and twisted together. The pins are rusted and the paper is brittle and yellow now. But the written words are still legible and they still tell the story of singularly blithe and carefree days.

None of the boys that I knew, either at Furnessville or at Joliet, had any interest in or inclination toward writing. No one in the whole countryside around Lone Oak had ever sold a single word for publication. The nearest approach was Gram who had seen some of her articles, contributed free, printed in *The Rural New Yorker.* It was my great good-fortune to spend the summers of these early years in the farmhouse where, more than anywhere else in that part of northern Indiana, my attempts at writing would be encouraged and appreciated.

Understanding and encouragement are sunshine and water to that frail plant, early ambition. They help the buried seed, the inner compulsion, get its foothold. Of course neither sunshine nor shower are effective without the seed. In the end, Robert Browning's *Andrea del Sarto* is right: "Incentives come from the soul's self, the rest avail not." "When," says Cyrano de Bergerac in Rostand's play, "I have made a line that sings . . . I pay myself a hundred times." It is this strange satisfaction, this joy of molding words into sentences which provides one of the most profound incentives to writing.

This satisfaction is an individual and almost lonely pleasure. It is difficult to explain and hard for others to understand. It reminds me, sometimes, of the joy a man I once interviewed for a magazine article found in whittling out little ducks. The year around, year in and year out, he carved from pieces of white pine miniature waterfowl—ducks in flight, ducks alighting, ducks feeding, ducks taking wing. It was his chief delight in life. As soon as he had a piece of white pine in one hand and a jackknife in the other, he was intensely happy.

"People," he told me as I was leaving him, "sometimes think I'm crazy. But they have no idea of the fun I'm having!"

·27·

THE BOX CAMERA

IN THE shade of the old oak tree, I scribbled down figures on the wooden top of a strawberry crate. A Sears, Roebuck catalogue lay in the grass beside me. I was busy figuring up exactly how many strawberries I would have to pick in order to obtain an object of my heart's desire.

Oftentimes, as I walked about the fields of Lone Oak or lay in the meadow-grass looking up at the drifting clouds or stole noiselessly along the mossy trails of the north woods, I had wished that I could record pictures of all the things I saw. Now I had decided to make this wish come true.

A few years before, when I was about eight years old, an uncle of mine had given me an oddity camera which had been produced at the time of the World's Columbian Exposition at Chicago, in 1893. It was the size and shape of a watch and had been designed to make miniature pictures, half as big as a postage stamp. Although no film was made to fit the camera, and its mechanism was then out of order, I used to carry it about with me, snapping imaginary pictures of birds' nests and wind-blown trees and long V's of autumn geese.

This summer, however, my heart was set on a real camera.

In the Sears, Roebuck catalogue I found listed a complete outfit—a box camera, a roll of film, a developing kit and printing material—all for $3.75. At that time of year the quickest source of money was the strawberry patch. Gramp paid me a cent and a half a quart for picking the berries. My figures on the white wood of the crate-top revealed that I would have to pick 250 quarts to obtain the needed sum.

The berries ran about eighty to the quart. That made a grand total of 20,000 strawberries which stood between me and the realization of my desire. I could visualize myself stooping over and picking off a berry and putting it in a box once, twice, three times, ten times, a hundred times, a thousand times, ten thousand times, twenty thousand times!

Nevertheless, I set to work. I asked Gramp to keep all my tally slips until I had the whole 250 quarts. Each evening I would ask him how the score stood. Progress was always disappointing; but the total mounted day by day. Finally the 250 quarts were picked and the money was mine. I made out the order carefully and printed the address on an envelope. Gramp came by while I was thus engaged. He volunteered:

"Better write large. Th' man may be deaf."

As soon as the mailman had picked up the letter the next morning, I began looking for the coming of the camera. Each succeeding morning, around nine o'clock, I would clamber up the hemlock tree in front of the farmhouse and peer eastward down the road to catch the first glimpse of the little white, covered-in cart in which the rural-delivery mailman brought letters and parcels from Michigan City. Day after day I hastily slid down again, my hands and bare feet black with the pitch of the resinous trunk, and raced to the mailbox as the cart pulled up in front of Lone Oak. And each day, for more than a week, disappointment awaited me.

After the top of the white cart had disappeared over Gunder's Hill I used to wander about the farm and along the marsh-paths and through the north woods spotting birds' nests and rabbit forms and woodchuck holes. As I walked I made lists of the innumerable pictures I would take as soon as the box camera came. On the ninth day it arrived.

I opened the package in haste. Half a dozen times I read the instructions. I was appalled at the complexity of even this simple mechanism. In handling it I seemed, as Gramp would say, "as awkward as a cow on skates." Fully half an hour had passed before I felt sufficient confidence to load in the roll of film. When the back was snapped shut and the film wound to "Number 1," I set forth—a camera-hunter in reality.

Beside the ditch bordering the cherry orchard a young cottontail had made its form. I had been training it on previous days for just this moment. Time after time I had approached slowly and silently until I was no more than four or five feet away. Then I had lifted an imaginary camera and had clicked an imaginary shutter. The rabbit was used to my presence. It would sit motionless for minutes at a time, watching me with round, unblinking eyes, its veined ears lying flat along its back.

Camera in hand, I now moved cautiously toward the cottontail. There was hardly a cloud in the sky. The sun was shining over my shoulder, just as the directions suggested. I squinted into the little rectangular window of the black box. The rabbit, sensing that something unusual was going on, lifted its ears. I pushed down the shutter-lever. At the metallic click, the cottontail was off, bolting away through the grass. But on my film, I felt sure, I had recorded a picture which would remain for years after the animal, itself, was no more.

Long before noon I had used my last film on a view of the house and the lone oak tree behind it. After dinner I picked strawberries with a fresh burst of enthusiasm. I realized that I would need many, many rolls of film to capture all the innumerable pictures I wanted to take.

I could hardly wait, that evening, for darkness to come. I read the instructions for developing the film over and over again. As soon as the supper dishes were washed, I laid my chemicals and trays out on the kitchen table and began hanging blankets over the windows. By half past eight it seemed dark enough to engage in the mysterious rite of photographic development.

First I mixed up my little packet of hypo and stirred into water the white powder from the tube of MQ developer. Then I lit a stub of a candle which fitted inside the red-cloth darkroom lantern. The dull reddish glow it emitted left me in almost complete darkness. I fumbled around for the roll of film, stripped off the paper, and began pumping the slippery strip up and down through the tray of developer. Eventually, against the dull glow of the red lantern, I was able to see thrilling evidences of pictures—lighter and darker patches on the film.

Although the strip, when finally dry, proved to be much over-developed and although black, light-struck patches marred the edges, the center section held pictures which we all could recognize. The rabbit, its ears erect and its round eyes alert, was the prize picture of the roll. It was the first of many thousand nature pictures which have provided interest and excitement during succeeding years.

My photographic fever continued all summer. I took under-exposed pictures in the depths of the north woods and over-exposed pictures in the glare of the sand-dunes. I snapped close-ups of moving animals and found only a blurred image on my film, and I photographed distant butterflies and saw them recorded no larger than pinheads on the resulting negatives. I learned by making mistakes.

There were so many pictures my box camera couldn't take, so many things too small to photograph or too fast to stop with a slow shutter speed, that disappointments mounted. However, even though only a small proportion of the hundreds of pictures I had seen vividly in my dreams ever materialized on film, the thrill of stalking wild creatures—camera in hand—and of seeing a long-desired picture take form before my eyes in the darkroom, left a lasting impression.

In later years other and better cameras followed this initial purchase. Each opened up new opportunities for close-ups or action shots. Each accompanied me on memorable trips afield, on expeditions that carried me tens of thousands of miles and resulted in a harvest of enjoyment as well as pictures. It was the black box of Lone Oak days—the camera that 20,000 strawberries purchased—that opened the door to all this later pleasure.

·28·

THE DEATH OF A TREE

FOR a great tree death comes as a gradual transformation. Its vitality ebbs slowly. Even when life has abandoned it entirely it remains a majestic thing. On some hilltop a dead tree may dominate the landscape for miles around. Alone among living things it retains its character and dignity after death. Plants wither; animals disintegrate. But a dead tree may be as arresting, as filled with personality, in death as it is in life. Even in its final moments, when the massive trunk lies prone and it has moldered into a ridge covered with mosses and fungi, it arrives at a fitting and a noble end. It enriches and refreshes the earth.

And later, as part of other green and growing things, it rises again.

The death of the great white oak which gave our Indiana homestead its name and which played such an important part in our daily lives was so gentle a transition that we never knew just when it ceased to be a living organism.

It had stood there, toward the sunset from the farmhouse, rooted in that same spot for 200 years or more. How many generations of red squirrels had rattled up and down its gray-black bark! How many generations of robins had sung from its upper branches! How many humans, from how many lands, had paused beneath its shade!

The passing of this venerable giant made a profound impression upon my young mind. Just what caused its death was then a mystery. Looking back, I believe the deep drainage ditches, which had been cut through the dune-country marshes a few years before, had lowered the water-table just sufficiently to affect the roots of the old oak. Millions of delicate root-tips were injured. As they began to wither, the whole vast underground system of nourishment broke down and the tree was no longer able to send sap to the upper branches.

Like a river flowing into a desert, the life stream of the tree dwindled and disappeared before it reached the topmost twigs. They died first. The leaf at the tip of each twig, the last to unfold, was the first to wither and fall. Then, little by little, the twig itself became dead and dry. This process of dissolution, in the manner of a movie run backward, reversed the development of growth. Just as, cell by cell, the twig had grown outward toward the tip, so now death spread, cell by cell, backward from the tip.

Sadly we watched the blight work from twig to branch, from smaller branch to larger branch, until the whole top of the tree was dead and bare. For years those dry, barkless upper branches remained intact. Their wood became gray and polished by the winds. When thunderstorms rolled over the farm from the northwest the dead branches shone like silver against the black and swollen sky. Robins and veeries sang from these lofty perches, gilded by the sunset long after the purple of advancing dusk filled the spaces below.

Then, one by one, their resiliency gone, the topmost limbs crashed to earth, carried away by the fury of stormwinds. In fragments and patches, bark from the upper trunk littered the ground below. The protecting skin of the tree was broken. In through the gaps poured a host of microscopic enemies, the organisms of decay.

Ghostly white fungus penetrated into the sap-wood. It worked its way downward along the unused tubes, those vertical channels through which had flowed the life-blood of the oak. The continued flow of this sap might have kept out the fungus. But sap rises only to branches clothed with leaves. As each limb became blighted and leafless, the saplevel dropped to the next living branch below. And close on the heels of this descending fluid followed the fungus. From branch to branch its silent, deadly descent continued.

Soft and flabby, so unsubstantial it can be crushed without apparent pressure between a thumb and forefinger, this pale fungus is yet able to penetrate through the hardest of woods. This amazing and paradoxical feat is accomplished by means of digestive enzymes which the fungus secretes and which dissolve the wood as strong acids might do. These fungus-enzymes, science has learned, are virtually the same as those produced by the single-celled protozoa which live in the bodies of the termites and enable those insects to digest the cellulose in wood.

Advancing in the form of thin white threads, which branch again and again, the fungus works its way from side to side as well as downward through the trunk of a dying tree. Beyond the reach of our eyes the fungus kept spreading within the body of the old oak, branching into a kind of vast, interlacing root-system of its own, pale and ghostly.

Behind the fungus, along the dead upper trunk, yellowhammers drummed on the dry wood. I saw them, with their chisel-bills, hewing out nesting holes which, in turn, admitted new organisms of decay. In effect, the dissolution of a great tree is like the slow turning of an immense wheel of life. Each stage of its decline and decay brings a whole new, interdependent population of dwellers and their parasites.

Even while the lower branches of the oak were still green, insect wreckers were already at work above them. First to arrive were the bark beetles. In the earliest stages their fare was the tender inner layer of the bark, the living bond between the trunk and its covering. As death spread downward in the oak, as freezing and storms loosened the bark, the beetles descended, foot by foot. Some of them left behind elaborate patterns, branching mazes of tunnels that took on the appearance of fantastic "thousand-leggers" engraved on wood.

During the winter when I was twelve years old a gale of abnormal force swept the Great Lakes region. Gusts reached almost hurricane proportions. Weakened by the work of the fungus, bacteria, woodpeckers, and beetles, the whole top of the tree snapped off some seventy feet from the ground. After that the progress of its dissolution was rapid.

Finally the last of the lower leaves disappeared. The green badge of life returned no more. On summer days the sound of the wind sweeping through the old oak had a winter shrillness. No more was there the rustling of a multitude of leaves above our hammock; no more was there the "plump!" of falling acorns. Leaves and acorns, life and progress, were at an end.

In the days that followed, as the bark loosened to the base, the wheel of life, which had its hub in the now-dead oak, grew larger.

I saw carpenter ants hurrying this way and that over the lower tree-trunk. Ichneumon flies, trailing deadly, drill-like ovipositors, hovered above the bark in search of buried larvae on which to lay their eggs. Carpenter bees, their black abdomens glistening like patent leather, bit their way into the dry wood of the dead branches. Click beetles and sow-bugs and small spiders found security beneath fragments of the loosened bark. And around the base of the tree swift-legged carabid beetles hunted their insect prey under cover of darkness.

Yellowish brown, the wood-flour of the powder-post beetles began to sift about the foot of the oak. It, in turn, attracted the larvae of the Darkling beetles. Thus, link by link, the chain of life expanded. To the expert eye the condition of the wood, the bark, the ground about the base of the oak—all told of the action of the inter-related forms of life attracted by the death and decay of a tree.

But below all this activity, beyond the power of human sight to detect, other changes were taking place. The underground root system, comprising almost as much wood as was visible in the tree rising above-ground, was also altering.

Fungus, entering the damaged root-tips or working downward from the infected trunk, followed the sap channels and hastened decay. The great main roots, spreading out as far as the widest branches of the tree itself, altered rapidly. Their fibers grew brittle; their old pliancy disappeared; their bark split and loosened. The breakdown of the upper tree found its counterpart, within the darkness of the earth, in the dissolution of the lower roots.

I remember well the day the great oak came down. I was fourteen at the time. Gramp had measured distances and planned his cutting operations in advance. He chopped away for fully half an hour before he had a V-shaped bite cut exactly in position to bring the trunk crashing in the place desired. Hours filled with the whine of the cross-cut saw followed.

Then came the great moment. A few last, quick strokes. A slow, deliberate swaying. The crack of parting fibers. Then a long "swo-o-sh!" that rose in pitch as the towering trunk arced downward at increasing speed. There followed a vast tumult of crashing, crackling sound; the dance of splintered branches; a haze of dead, swirling grass. Then a slow settling of small objects and silence. All was over. Lone oak was gone.

Gram, I remember, brushed away what she remarked was dust in her eyes with a corner of her apron and went inside. She had known and loved that one great tree since she had come to the farm as a bride of sixteen. She had seen it under all conditions and through eyes colored by many moods. Her children had grown up under its shadow and I, a grandchild, had known its shade. Its passing was like the passing of an old, old friend. For all of us there seemed an empty space in our sky in the days that followed.

Gramp and I set to work, attacking the fallen giant. Great piles of cordwood, mounds of broken branches for kindling, grew around the prostrate trunk as the weeks went by. Eventually only the huge, circular table of the low stump remained—reddish brown and slowly dissolving into dust.

For two winters wood from the old oak fed the kitchen range and the dining-room stove. It had a clean, well-seasoned smell. And it burned with a clear and leaping flame, continuing—unlike the quickly consumed poplar and elm—for an admirable length of time. Like the old tree itself, the fibers of these sticks had character and endurance to the very end.

·29·

CHRISTMAS EVE

SNOW covered the stump of the old oak tree. Drifts curved across the woodyard, half encircled the spring. They lay deep along the northern fringe of the woods and the distant dunes were glistening white instead of shining gold. In an unbroken blanket the snow stretched across the lower forty where *The Dragonette* had stood. It clogged the ditches; turned the marsh into a wide, level plain of whiteness; ran up one side of the cornshocks which, like men with their hands in their pockets, stood hunched along the horizon.

It was the day before Christmas and to my young eyes

the whole dune country seemed like an immense cake covered with a thick layer of frosting.

Under the drifting plume of woodsmoke rising from the Lone Oak chimney great activity was in progress. All the daughters of the family were home and everybody seemed cooking at once. There was the clatter of crockery and the whir of egg-beaters and the crackling and snapping of a roaring kitchen fire. Dates were being pitted, stuffed with nuts, and rolled in confectioner's sugar. Walnut fudge and heavenly-hash candy cooled on plates in the pantry. Friedcakes were bobbing about and turning a golden brown in a kettle of bubbling lard. And, at the back of the range, popcorn—grown in Gramp's own fields—volleyed against the tin lid of an iron skillet.

Popcorn was an important item on the list of materials used at Christmastime. Strung on white cotton thread, with the aid of a needle, it provided decorations for the tree. Buttered and salted, it was the chief "nibbling" food which kept Gramp and me alive from meal to meal during the Yuletide excitement. With sorghum molasses, it was molded into popcorn balls. And, as "Popcorn Mound," it appeared with white icing over it and was cut like a cake with a very sharp knife.

I sat in one corner of the kitchen, near the windows, and cracked nuts on a flatiron. The day before Gramp and I had plowed through the drifts to the north woods and after much deliberation had selected a well-formed spruce as our Christmas tree. It was between seven and eight feet high. I had dragged it home through the snow, chattering incessantly in my excitement.

I snickered now when I recalled what Gramp had said. As soon as he could get a word in edgewise, he had observed: "Edwin, ef y' don't keep yer mouth shut, y'll freeze yer tongue an' give yer teeth a sleigh-ride!"

Stamping our feet and shaking the snow from the green boughs of the spruce, we had brought the tree indoors and had established it in a corner of the dining room. It stood there now, completely decorated with strings of popcorn and cranberries, polished apples and candy fish. In that same spot had stood every Christmas tree that I recalled, from the earliest I remembered to this—my last at Lone Oak.

Dinnertime came and went. Gramp and I were fed hastily on bean soup and shooed out of the kitchen. We began playing checkers on the dining-room table. From time to time I would leave the game, stick my head out in the kitchen, and inquire:

"Is there anything I can do to help?"

Usually the answer was: "No."

But when it was affirmative I jumped to be of assistance.

"Y' certainly are polite ez a basket o' chips today!" Gramp remarked.

Because the house warmed up slowly on winter mornings, we always distributed the presents at Lone Oak on Christmas Eve. Already they lay piled in their holiday wrappings under the tree in the corner. I studied them closely at intervals. At the back of the pile was a large, irregular object wrapped in red and green paper. I knew what that was. It was a new clothes-wringer for Gram from my father and mother. My own presents were, in the main, impenetrable mysteries. There was one exception. This was a small, heavy box. I was sure it contained a jackknife. Every Christmas somebody gave me a new jackknife, which, invariably, I lost before the next Christmas arrived.

The hours of the afternoon dragged by and Gramp and I began to think of chores. As I gathered the eggs and carried in armloads of stove-wood, my shoes squeaked on the dry snow and my breath billowed out in white clouds of vapor. Cornstalks, stripped of their leaves, littered the trampled snow of the barnyard. The strawstack, where I forked out fresh bedding for the horses, had taken on the appearance of a giant, thick-stemmed mushroom from the rubbing of the cattle around its base. Snow, piled deeply on its top, enhanced the resemblance. At the corncrib I picked out an extra ration of the largest yellow ears. These I distributed as a Christmas present to Deck, Colty, and Dolly in the warm and pungent interior of their stable. They, too, got their presents on Christmas Eve.

By the time Gramp and I stamped into the kitchen again, supper was waiting on the dining-room table. I hurried through it, hardly tasting what I ate until I reached the dessert—a dish of sweet and juicy blackberries, the product of our own labors the summer before. With all the girls helping, the dishes were washed, wiped, and whisked into the cupboard in an amazingly short space of time. I brought a jug of sweet cider and a pan of

Northern Spy apples from the cellar. They took their place beside the plates of candy and the bowls of popcorn on the dining-room table. We were all ready for the main excitement of the day: the opening of the presents.

From the time I was six or seven we had followed the same time-honored procedure. Each grown person sat in a different part of the room while I delivered the presents, one at a time in rotation. After each round I opened a present of my own.

The first box I unwrapped contained a dud—a necktie. Next came a surprise, a pocket instrument called a "Telemeter." According to the instructions, if I looked through it at a distant object, an indicator would tell me how far away the object was. I became so engrossed in this gadget that I forgot there were other presents still to be delivered until I heard Gramp saying:

"I guess Santa Claus hez had a lapse o' memory."

Two other presents I received that night stand out in my mind. One was a set of wood-carving tools. Each tool had a polished walnut handle and they all were contained in a sturdy box with a sliding top. The second present was the real prize of the evening. It was a pocket-guide to the birds. The cover carried the picture of a red-headed woodpecker and within were paintings of more than 190 birds, with the range, habits, and other data given about each.

The final present of all—after little mounds of string and discarded wrapping paper had grown in size beside each chair—was a large pasteboard box. It was covered with white tissue-paper and on top was a poinsettia cut from red paper. It carried the printed inscription:

"TO ALL FROM ALL."

Within the box was an assortment of home-made candies, preserved fruits, and little tissue-paper bundles of nut-meats. In the course of its preparation, I had sampled each of the sweetmeats and so now went, like a bee to a flower, to my preferences.

When this present "to all" had made its rounds, we each examined the presents the others had received. The handkerchiefs, doilies, aprons, hand-embroidered towels, and hand-painted china all left me lukewarm. The books, which Gram would read aloud in the evenings to come, stirred my interest. But it was an elaborate "pyrography" set which my aunt Winnifred had received which absorbed me to the exclusion of everything else.

This outfit was used for burning designs into wood. A glass container filled with wood-alcohol supplied fuel. A rubber bulb pumped up air-pressure and fed the alcohol to a metal point to keep it red-hot. In the days that followed we all tried our hand at burning floral and bird designs in the tops of boxes and on the flat surfaces of smooth boards. The smell of alcohol and wood-smoke filled the house for hours on end. This outfit, together with my carving set—which left evidences of its use in the form of chips and shavings on the kitchen floor—provided the most amusement for indoor hours during succeeding days.

By a little after nine o'clock, the popcorn was gone, the Northern Spy apples had been reduced to cores, mining operations had left gaps and gullies in the box of candy, and the cider jug was empty. Coming events had cast no shadow over our Christmas fun.

Christmas Day, with its bountiful dinner, lay just ahead, and beyond that days of leisure, of coasting, of skating on the wide marsh ditch, of seeing the sights of the winter fields. More than a week of freedom still remained. But as I placed my bird book and my carving tools on the back of the kitchen table and prepared to climb the stairs to bed, there came a sudden twinge of sadness, a rebound from the elation of the day. The peak of the year was past. Christmas Eve was over.

· 30 ·

THE JOURNEY

LONE OAK days came to their end almost at the same time that the golden age of boyhood drew to a close.

I was nearing my sixteenth year and the world had turned serious. I was studying hard in high school, saving my money, even combing my hair. Determined some day to be a writer, I was making earnest, if somewhat ineffective, efforts to improve my spelling. I had begun to budget my time and to pin little schedules for the day on the walls of my room.

In the autumn of that year I had been greatly impressed by the story of King Alfred the Great and his colored candles. As I heard the tale, King Alfred had organized his day by burning candles formed of sections of colored tallow. He would devote himself to one study as long as the candle burned through blue tallow, to another task when the tallow was red, to another when it was green, and so on. I set out to follow suit. At first I tried to put colored bands around a wax candle with watercolors. Then I jumped ahead a thousand years and relied on my Ingersoll dollar-watch. Sloth and Indolence and Careless Habits of the Past were ranged against me and I often despaired of progress.

I remember I once lugged home from the ivy-covered, gray-limestone building of the Joliet Public Library a huge volume on the development of will power. Its pages depressed me greatly. They led me to the conclusion that I had been born without any will power at all.

At the ends of the various sections of this book there were suggested exercises for strengthening the will. The one which I remember most clearly related to the cultivation of persistence. First, you snarled up a ball of yarn and then, by persistent effort, you straightened out the tangle. Choosing an afternoon when I was alone in the house, I set about testing my perseverance. I was unable to find a ball of yarn, so I used a spool of silk. Conscientiously I snarled up the fine thread until it looked like a mouse's nest. Then I gave my persistence a workout—and what a workout!

I soon found that I needed more room than the desktop and stretched out on the dining-room carpet. The silk

I had chosen was dark blue. The carpet had light and dark areas in its pattern. As I pulled out the thread-ends, the silk "disappeared" wherever it lay on the darker portions of the pattern and I would reach for it repeatedly before I could pick it up. Even without this handicap my troubles would have been sufficient.

I had expected to have the thread back on the spool before my mother came home from shopping. Instead I was snarled in silk like the proverbial kitten when she arrived. I was in the same condition when my father reached home from work. The gas-lights went on and I pulled out a thousand and one wrong loops and threads and the snarl remained.

During supper I was struck by a sudden revelation. It didn't matter, except to my mother who was losing a spool of silk, whether I ever unraveled the snarl or not. I had kept at it for hours and that fact alone proved I had persistence. I went gaily to bed that night, feeling that my time had not been wasted.

One other indication of the serious trend of the times was the fact that calisthenics had come into their own. I walked with my shoulders thrown back and my chest out. I ate raw carrots. I drank a glass of hot water before breakfast. Also I began looking at myself in the mirror from time to time and was amazed, as almost invariably I have been since, at the difference between the way I looked on the outside and the way I felt on the inside.

When summer came, I told myself, there would be no more loafing at Lone Oak. I would work conscientiously.

I would save the money earned from strawberry picking, from fallen apples, from Early Rose potatoes. I would act the part of a man. Childhood was over, a thing of the past.

It was—indeed. Even while such thoughts were running through my mind, as I lay in bed on a January night, Gramp was piling wood into the great dining-room stove at Lone Oak, banking the roaring fire before he went to bed. So bitter was the cold outside that he left the draft partially on for the night. During the hours of darkness, the wind rose in violence. The metal of the stove grew red and sparks streamed upward through the pipe.

At three o'clock in the morning Gram awoke coughing. The ground-floor bedroom was thick with drifting woodsmoke. She could hear the rush of flames and the crackle of burning wood. Gramp woke up and jumped from bed. He swung open the kitchen door. The eastern end of the house was filled with sheets of red and yellow flame.

A moment later Gramp was forcing up one of the bedroom windows and pushing back the heavy green shutters outside. Pulling on their shoes and throwing quilts around their shoulders, they stepped out into the below-zero wind and the foot-deep snow.

Under his arm Gramp had a black walnut box. For more than forty years that wooden box had rested each night on the floor under the head of his bed. It contained all the papers of value he owned—the deed to the farm, the insurance policies, his Civil War papers, his ready cash. A hundred times he had said:

"Ef th' house ever catches fire, the first thing I'll grab

will be that box!"

They had fled just in time. Already streamers of fire were running across the western roof. With the knife-edged wind cutting to the marrow of their bones, they waded through drifts, tinted red by the soaring flames, to the house of their nearest neighbor.

There, warmed by the stove and revived by steaming coffee, they watched the home they had known so long settle into a mass of glowing embers. The house had followed the oak. When the sun rose there seemed an empty place on the horizon, just as there had seemed an empty space in the sky when the old tree came down.

As soon as we heard of the fire, I took the train for Furnessville to bring Gramp and Gram to Joliet. They were well past seventy; yet they showed no ill-effects from their tramp through wind and snow.

"I remember once saying," Gram recalled, "that I couldn't see why people got excited in a fire. I was sure I would keep calm. But it came so suddenly that I don't know whether I stayed cool or not."

"Wal, yer feet stayed cool," Gramp told her. "They were in th' snow!"

We poked among the ruins. At one place we found the silverware, melted into a gray blob of metal. At another place we discovered blackened fragments of the steel dictionary-stand in the parlor. But the dictionary, with its pictures of butterflies, birds, and airplanes, was gone forever—as were so many of the other old, familiar objects. Gramp's best hat had perished on the corner of a picture-frame and the lamp, beside which Gram had read on so many summer evenings, had changed into a formless lump of melted glass.

For a while the old folks talked of rebuilding on the brick foundation of the homestead. Then they had a chance to sell the farm as it stood. They took it. Afterward Gramp and Gram journeyed 200 miles and retired to well-earned leisure, spending most of the rest of their lives in happy years at the home of their daughter, Elizabeth, in Richmond, Ind. There, during the four years I was attending Earlham College, we were united once more.

An old Hawaiian proverb says that the earth is a mother that never dies. So it is that Lone Oak Farm has gone on the same, even though "time and the world are ever in flight." Its face has altered with the years. But the old fields are there. The spring and the mossy north woods and the arid Field of the Serpents are as they were. And the far dunes still lift their gold to the summer sun beyond the treetops.

Even today, if you look south from a speeding Michigan Central train, a mile or so east of the old station of Furnessville, you can see, for a fleeting instant, the dark and slender spire of a cedar tree. It stands rooted, like a living memorial shaft, beside the spot where once the Lone Oak gate stood ready to swing open at my touch.

LONE OAK
Forty Years After

· 31 ·

THE GOLD WATCH

MORE than forty years have now passed since the great oak came crashing down. Forty winters have come and gone since the cold night when the farmhouse burned. As I write these words, Gramp's gold watch, the source of so many loans in his lean years, lies on my desk beside me. I lift it. It is solid, weighing more than a quarter of a pound. I hold it cupped in my hand. It, too, was at Lone Oak. It, too, shared all those early years that return with such vividness to my mind.

"If it rains," Gramp used to say when the summer sky would darken, "we'll do what they do in Spain."

"What's that?" I would ask.

"Let it rain!"

Sometimes on mornings when we would return from dew-wet meadows with milkpails filled with mushrooms, we all would set to work peeling off the tough outer skins. This was unexciting work for Gramp. With his huge jack-knife he would peel off half the mushroom with the skin. To Gram's remonstrances he would reply:

"I'm jest too strong fer this work."

Long before I arrived on the scene, a custom in the dune country, my mother once recalled, was telling fortunes by looking into one of the chapters of the Book of Proverbs and choosing the verse number that corresponded to the day of birth. Everyone at Lone Oak remembered how Gramp's verse ended:

"Give me neither poverty nor riches; feed me with food convenient for me."

In the matter of food he was always a pioneer. He tried new dishes. He planted new crops. He was the only farmer I ever heard of who tried to raise peanuts in the sand dunes. Several rows at the edge of the garden produced a scanty crop of rather small nuts. Gram roasted them on the range. Gramp rationed them out with a special flourish.

There was a year when he decided he could get maple syrup from the big maple tree that grew north of the hay-field where Dolly achieved a kind of immortality by being the one-horsepower motor of *The Dragonette.* He brought home nearly a pailful of sap and boiled it on the back of the kitchen range. From time to time he would cool and sip a few drops of the liquid. Each time he would hastily add a little more brown sugar. The boiling and the sugar-adding went on hour after hour. In the end he proudly exhibited a teacupful or so of syrup for his pancakes.

"This is mighty sweet maple syrup," he reported complacently the next morning.

"It would be even sweeter," Gram reminded him, "if you'd put in more sugar."

Whenever he was away from home, Gramp kept his eyes peeled for new foods. Once when he was a small boy eating with relatives, he remembered replying to an invitation to help himself to the potatoes:

"No thank y'. I don't want any potatoes. We hev potatoes at home."

At any gathering where a plate of sandwiches went around for a second or third time—or, for that matter, a fourth or fifth time—Gramp was wont to remark:

"I b'lieve I will hev another, thank y'. I was so busy talkin' I forgot t' taste that last one."

He was always polite to cooks. And if anything struck his fancy at the table he was quick to say so. In contrast, some of the other farmers of the region stolidly ate whatever was set before them without comment. The wife of one of them observed earnestly to Gram one day:

"Even a little grumblin' would be comfortin'."

Gramp's father was an expert woodsman. Six feet, two inches tall, he was tireless in the forest, able to fell trees from dawn to dusk day after day. He came west to Indiana with his four motherless children because he heard the forests were being cleared around the southern end of Lake Michigan. Hardly had he settled there when one disaster after another overwhelmed him. In a sawmill accident his left hand was severed at the wrist. No longer able to chop down trees, he still worked in the woods. Using his right arm alone, he split logs into cordwood. To help in this work he kept his axe ground almost to razor sharpness. One winter day of bitter cold this axe glanced on a piece of hard hickory. The blade buried itself just below his left knee. Never again was he able to walk.

In so short a time he was reduced from a giant who never tired to a one-handed cripple dragging himself about on crutches. But even then he continued working with trees. He planted an apple orchard. He began experimenting with grafting. People in the 1870's drove for many miles to see one of his trees with sweet apples growing on one side and sour apples on the other. His were the first grafted trees of the dune country. Another feature of his orchard famous in pioneer times was his Twenty-Ounce Pippin. It never produced an apple that weighed less than a pound.

In consequence of the misfortunes that befell his father, Gramp began working as a hired hand on a farm when he was about twelve years old. His wages were eight dollars a month. Seventy years later he could recall one of his first days at the home of his employer.

The man called to his dog:

"Come here!"

The dog sat still.

"Come here, I tell y'!"

The dog got up, stretched, ambled away in the opposite direction.

"Go on over there!" the man shouted after him. "I *will* hev y' mind!"

In the dune country, when I was young, there was a number of German and Polish farmers who had recently come to America. Their knowledge of English was often scanty. When Gramp spoke to one of these neighbors, we noticed, he always talked extra loud. For years a first English sentence of one of these newcomers remained a saying in the dunes. It was:

"Nobody so good like I."

Because of the different nationalities that emigrated to the region, it became a kind of melting pot of Old World superstitions. I have recalled some of these odd beliefs in a previous chapter. Others were just as widely held. A dropped pin, for example, was often examined closely. If it pointed toward the finder it meant good luck was on the way. For rheumatism the thing to do was to carry a small potato in a coat pocket. As the potato dried and shriveled, rheumatic pains would disappear. Hair combed out by women was supposed to be discarded where birds would not find it. For if such strands were woven into a nest, it was thought, the original owner would suffer from headaches until the young birds had flown away. Two other superstitions of the time no doubt aided in the disposal of burned toast and in getting daughters up and at work early in the morning. These were the beliefs that aids to a fine complexion were eating charred toast and washing the face in the earliest dew of dawn.

Distinct from these superstitions of her neighbors were the innumerable home remedies I remember Gram used in times of illness. Whenever I developed a sore throat she bound around my neck, inside a strip of flannel, a piece of salt pork sprinkled with pepper. My chest colds were met with a generous poultice of hot fried onions. My burns received first the white of an egg, then a coating of lard, followed later by an application of flour. In early days before my time, quinine was swallowed in quantity every summer to combat the ague. To speed it on its way the white powder was often placed between bits of the bark of slippery elm. And when Gram's eyes became inflamed from the sun or from reading she sought relief in a soothing poultice of wet tea leaves.

As I run back over these random memories stirred to life by Gramp's worn gold watch lying beside me, it occurs to me that I have never given proper recognition to an important influence in those early days. This is the card game of "Authors." We played it often when I was small. Pictures on the cards of Emerson, Scott, Poe and Wordsworth, and, even more, the scenes relating to their masterpieces, became indelibly imprinted on my mind. The wild glens of Scotland, the Lake Country of Wordsworth, a lonely seashore illustrating one of Poe's poems—these I still remember. The lasting curiosity they aroused played a part, no doubt, in making books so important an element in my later life.

It is now a cause of considerable regret that nobody ever wrote down all the stories Gram made up and told in the dusk or dark when she put the children to bed. One tale, now but a vaguely remembered delight of long ago, continued like a serial story night after night. In this imaginary account the central character was the squirrel that buried the acorn that produced the great Lone Oak tree.

·32·

FLEA-SKINNERS

"HE'D skin a flea fer its hide an' tallow!"

Thus Gramp sometimes described three or four of the tighter-fisted inhabitants of the dune country. In those days when hard cash was scarce and paper currency was even scarcer, pennies were watched in all the farmhouses of the region. But they were watched more closely in some than in others.

In the homes of the flea-skinners postage stamps, for example, always came in for a special scrutiny.

"I al'ays say t' my girls," a neighbor confided to Gram, "never t' write t' any young feller who won't pay th' postage. He ain't serious."

Once Gramp and I started early for town in the cracker wagon. As usual, he called:

"All aboard, Edwin—if y' can't get a board git a plank!"

Half way to Michigan City he pulled up to pass the time of day with the owner of a large farm. As he was clucking to Deck and Colty and we were starting off again the farmer's wife asked him to mail a letter to her mother in South Dakota.

"Look at that!" the farmer exclaimed. "*Another* letter! *Another* stamp! She writes t' her folks an' says: 'We're all well. Hope you're th' same.' A week later they write back: 'So glad you're all well. We are too. Write again soon.' An' then right off th' bat she writes another letter an' starts the whole blamed thing all over again. *Be sure to write soon!* It's a plumb waste o' money!"

A far greater menace than postage stamps, however, was posed by the insatiable appetites of the hired men.

"T' hear old Billy talk," Gramp once reported as we were sitting down to supper, "you'd think his hired men had all lost their appetites—an' found the appetites o' wolves."

Battles and skirmishes, ruses and flank movements were engaged in at the tables of the flea-skinners. In one house fresh bread appeared on the table only at the very end of a meal. Then it was left out to dry and so become less palatable before the next meal. At another place the consumption of butter was greatly reduced by the ingenuity of the housewife. Each day she carefully molded it into a round ball. Then just before she set it on the table she heated the plate so the butter would skid and roll when anyone tried to cut off a piece. This scheme worked until a new hired man appeared. After politely chasing the butter around the plate with his table knife, he stood up, reached into his back pocket and said:

"Here's a knife that ain't *never* ashamed!"

With that he opened the blade of a huge jackknife, speared the ball and held it down while he sliced off a generous chunk.

Sometimes in the dunes the same household would contain one easy-going person and one driver. A hundred times the same exchange occurred between two brothers on a farm a mile or so from Lone Oak.

"I'll have no idle flesh around me!" the driver-brother would shout.

"My sweat," the easy-going brother would reply, "is worth a dollar a drop."

On our way to Michigan City Gramp would sometimes point out the house of "the man who threw his hat in the kitchen door." He had married a wife from the other side of Burdick. She was the high-tempered driver of the family. In time it became his habit to discover storm signals by standing outside the kitchen and throwing his hat inside. If it didn't come flying out again, it was safe for him to go in.

How money was spent, or not spent, was a favorite topic around the stove at Lewrey's Store. Over and over again the tale was told of the young man who came back to Furnessville after working for a year in Chicago. He climbed down from the train, resplendent in a scarlet necktie. He casually pulled from his pocket a ten-dollar bill. He rolled it up, ignited one end, lit his cigar with it and tossed the charred remnant away. It was the gesture of a lifetime. And it was the only thing he was remembered for during a generation of dune-country life.

Then there was Lew Payne and his licorice.

Lew had come west in the Fifties, arriving a few years before Gramp. His farm was just above the Furnessville station. Some of the promptness of the trains that came and went on schedule seemed to enter his makeup. Every Sunday night, precisely at seven o'clock, he and his wife would walk next door to visit Aunt Mary. Promptly on the dot of nine he would clap on his hat and they would start back along the path to home.

His wife was noted all through the countryside as the first woman to have her wash on the line Monday mornings. In later years, as the frailties of age increased, she maintained this distinction by dipping two clean sheets in water and hanging them out as soon as she arose. Then, with her reputation secure, she could go on with her regular washing at leisure. A second characteristic of her daily life was her promptness in washing dishes. Her repeated assertion was:

"I can't abide a dirty dish."

So, even when there was company, the dishes would

be whisked away from under the noses of the visitors as soon as they had taken their last bites. Sometimes they would still be chewing when the clatter of washing dishes would arise from the kitchen.

Lew Payne was the proud possessor of the longest white beard in the dune country. He used to stroke it meditatively as he related how, when he was fifteen years old, he went to Valparaiso with his first month's salary in his pocket. For half a day he walked up and down the streets looking in the store windows. He couldn't decide what to get. Finally he went into a drugstore and bought five dollars' worth of licorice.

"An' fer a fact," he used to end his recital, "I never really cared much fer licorice since."

In money matters Gramp had only one peculiarity. At the end of each month, when he stopped at Lewrey's Store to settle up his bill, he would invariably leave a small amount unpaid. As long as he lived at Lone Oak, in spite of all of Gram's remonstrances and cajolery, even at harvest time when he was his wealthiest, he always left a little indebtedness on the books.

"Why in heaven's name," Gram would demand indignantly, "don't y' pay it *all?* Then y' won't owe anybody anything."

"Nope," I would always hear Gramp reply, "Ez long ez I owe a little, I git better service."

·33·

LONE OAK RETURN

FAR from Lone Oak in space and in time, on a recent day in the New York Public Library, I opened the bound volume of a long-defunct magazine. Forty-four years had passed since that stormy afternoon when I helped anchor down the flying boat on the Michigan City beach. Yet the scene returned, each detail vivid. For in this aging publication I came upon recollections of that first air-and-water race set down by the owner of the winged boat, J. B. R. Verplanck.

He recalled flying through the smoke of the Gary steel mills and coming out into the wonderful air of the dunes.

It was rich with the scent of sweet ferns or "a sort of Indiana heather." Welcomed by an enormous crowd and a white flag waved vigorously, he and Beckwith Havens landed at Michigan City. "The storm that had been threatening all afternoon," he wrote, "broke on us with terrific fury. The beach was cleared in an instant and we began the fight of our lives to keep the old boat from starting on a cruise over the sand dunes. At first we had two volunteers. But after getting soaked they resigned in favor of *one small boy.*"

Those italics are here contributed, so many years later, by that same "one small boy."

Not long after *Dune Boy* was first published in the war-year of 1943, I received a note from Beckwith Havens. A relative had given him the book for Christmas. At the time he was in charge of a naval flying school on Long Island and he invited me to spend a Sunday afternoon with him. I found him a slender, handsome man with graying hair. As we talked he recalled some of the adventures of the race after the dunes had been left behind.

Once, beyond the Straits of Mackinac, rain began falling from low-hanging clouds. Verplanck, who had been studying a map outspread on his knees, crawled into the nose of the flying boat to keep dry. Havens pulled back the wheel and climbed up through the clouds into brilliant sunshine above. He rapped on the hull and Verplanck came out. Just as they began to enjoy the beauty of the cloudscape around them the engine stopped. Fuel was gone. Down they went into the clouds again, descending in a steep glide. They were uncertain whether land or water lay below them. Bursting out of the vapor they found themselves above the lake a mile or so from shore. With the aid of a paddle, Havens worked the craft to the beach and then started on a ten-mile hike for gasoline.

In addition to its mention of the sky race in which he had participated, Havens found another particular link with my book. He, too, as a small boy, had known freedom and escape from town on his grandfather's farm. It lay up the Hudson River from New York City. There, too, just as at Lone Oak, that happy period came to an end when the old farmhouse burned to the ground.

A year or two before *Dune Boy* was written, I was driving back to the Lone Oak region when I stopped for lunch at La Porte. In the telephone book I came, by a lucky chance, upon the name "Verne Bradfield." The Verne I had known had been lost track of soon after he moved to Sunbury, Ohio, in 1910. I had heard indirectly that he had been killed in the First World War. But the name was so unusual I dropped a note to the La Porte Verne. He was indeed my boyhood friend. Later I stopped to see him. After so many years, we re-lived for an hour or two all the innumerable small adventures of our Lone Oak days. At the time he was working in a New York Central mail-car running between Chicago and Cleveland. Dewey Gunder, my other boyhood companion, is also a railroad man, the engineer of a crack Michigan Central express on the Detroit-Chicago run.

One way, I have discovered, to learn more about the events of your childhood is to write a book about them. People from as far away as California wrote in sending their recollections of the dune country or their remembrances of the Ways. One reader invited me to visit his home in Glengarry, Idaho, 2,000 miles away. Another wanted me to attend a party in a Riverside Drive apartment and tell the story of the mouse pelts to one of her guests, a Fifth Avenue furrier. A United States Senator wrote that during vacations in the dunes he used to read the book aloud to his young daughter. And the man who was, at one time, head of all the subways in New York City recalled that he had been the dispatcher in the "lighted brick tower" at Michigan City about the time Smith Hill was killed.

After an Armed Services Edition of more than 100,000 copies of the book had been distributed during the war, I heard from many men who had read it amid strange surroundings. One had been riding a bomber being ferried to England. Another had been resting in a small Burma village after a battle. A third had been sitting in a castle on the Rhine. A fourth had been sweating in the jungles of a South Pacific island where Seabees were building an airstrip.

But, in some ways, the person who followed the story under the most unusual circumstances of all was a six-year-old boy. His mother gave him the book for Christmas. Together they read it in the very house where Verne

Bradfield had lived, across the road from Lone Oak. And as they came to each successive chapter they visited the exact spots mentioned—the North Woods, the spring, The Island, the old apple orchard, the lower field where *The Dragonette* flew.

Another reader who visited the actual places mentioned in the book lived in Wilmette, Illinois. He wrote that he had typed out a list of every place and every person mentioned in *Dune Boy*. Carrying it in the glove compartment of his car, he drove across the Indiana line each weekend. He followed the back-country roads. He talked with local residents. He compared the names on tombstones in country cemeteries with those on his list. Thus, making trip after trip, he narrowed down the area until he located The Island, the spring, the foundation bricks of the farmhouse and the old cedar tree close to the spot where the gate once stood.

The first time I returned to the dunes after the book appeared I found I had received no small honor: a dog had been named after me. The operator of the Wilson Shelter Canteen in the Indiana Dunes State Park had come upon a half-starved puppy on one of the trails. He fed it and took it home. When he sought a name for it he remembered a book he had just been reading. He called it Dune Boy.

As I look back on my early years I know that my boyhood was not, as boyhood is supposed to be, the happiest time of my life. But all the days at Lone Oak were like golden islands in a stormy sea. So they appeared then.

So they seem now. Each memory of them might well begin: "Once upon a wonderful time . . ."

My last Lone Oak return—a century after Gramp came west, forty years after the farmhouse burned, a dozen years after *Dune Boy* first appeared in print—occurred two springs ago as this is written.

I found the land of the dunes today is something of a paradox. As many as 10,000 persons come to the lake shore of the Indiana Dunes State Park on a Fourth of July. Yet in the region around foxes have come back and even deer are occasionally seen. Great superhighways now carry their rivers of traffic to the north and south of Lone Oak. Yet its immediate surroundings lie in a kind of quiet backwater. There are changes, of course. But curiously it is less the change than the lack of change that is impressive.

The country road is still dusty, still narrow, still winding. The houses where Dewey and Verne once lived are almost unchanged. Years of cutting have thinned the North Woods and I hunted in vain for the mossy hollow where the wintergreens once grew. But to the south the Père Marquette Railroad formed the same stable landmark bordered by the same ditches where Dewey and I once caught crayfish and dined on their tails boiled over a campfire in a blackened tin-can.

And so, that day, I came once more to the old cedar tree. Always when I return to the dunes I examine this one tree closely. I note the changes of the years as one views a failing friend with affectionate concern. Half way to the top now the trunk was smoothly bare. A few of the upper twigs appeared lifeless and dry. But over most of its topmost limbs the tree still remained darkly, richly green. Before I left I gazed for a long time at those enduring branches. Each was a living link with remembered days. Each was a symbol of my long farewell to Lone Oak.

The author with a tandem glider built in 1912.

The hayfield where *The Dragonette* flew.

The old farmhouse at Lone Oak. This was one of the first pictures taken with the box camera earned by picking strawberries.

DUNE
SCENE